Breathless

Peter spun around in his chair, flicked a switch and checked a turntable. He grabbed two pairs of lightweight earphones and hung one around his neck.

"You need to wear these."

Peter leaned toward her. Lisa started to take the earphones from him, but instead he moved closer and put them over her ears himself. His face was very close to hers. Again he stopped and stared at her with the strangest, searching look. Lisa wasn't sure what it meant, but it made her feel flushed and breathless.

Peter backed away, cleared his throat, then spun around again to take out a record. Finally he flipped on the microphone with one graceful motion.

"Hello, Cardinals. This is Peter Lacey, your man at WKND here with another day of homecoming specials. This week I've been interviewing the candidates for junior princess. Today we have Lisa Chang. Hello Lisa," Peter looked at Lisa to let her know it was her turn to talk.

Lisa took a deep breath and prepared herself.

COUPLES

Books from Scholastic
in the **Couples** series:

FIRE AND ICE

COUPLES

FIRE AND ICE

By Linda A. Cooney

SCHOLASTIC INC.
New York Toronto London Auckland Sydney

ISBN 0-590-33391-7

16 15 14 13 12 11 10 9 8 7 6 5   1 2 3 4 5/9

Printed in the U.S.A.   01

FIRE AND ICE

Chapter 1

*T*here was a moment of stunned silence. The intensity of the lights made the ice glisten and sparkle with an unearthly glow. Lisa Chang's heart beat very fast, and she could feel the energy flowing through her body. As she heard the final chord of "Rhapsody in Blue," she threw she arms over her head. Instantly the crowd exploded with shouts and cheers. The ecstatic roars echoed off the concrete walls of the ice rink. Lisa continued to stand in the middle of the ice and hold her dramatic pose. The cheering grew even louder.

Lisa looked up into the stands and saw her mother and father in the front row. They were waving tiny American flags and it looked like her mother was laughing and crying at the same time. Next to them was Mr. Helde, Lisa's longtime skating teacher. He was clapping his large hands together and eyeing the judges expectantly. Lisa turned to the other side of the bleachers and picked out two of her old friends. Phoebe Hall and Chris Austin were jumping up and down. When they saw Lisa look their way, they waved and screamed her name. Surrounding Phoebe and Chris were six or seven other kids from their crowd at school. Those were kids that Lisa didn't recognize. But they obviously knew her, and they were as wild with excitement as Phoebe and Chris.

Breathless, Lisa skated to the edge of the rink to wait for her scores. There was no reason to be afraid. In her years as a figure skater she had never executed a freestyle routine so perfectly. She had not missed a single leap, jump, or spin, and she had put her soul into every second of the performance. She had shared with the audience the incredible joy of flying and gliding over the ice.

Her scores came up. Perfect sixes! One after another they lit up on the electronic scoreboard, and each time the audience gasped and the applause swelled. She knew that soon she would close her eyes and listen to "The Star Spangled Banner" and it would sound like the most beautiful piece of music she had ever heard.

And when they placed that gold medal around her neck it would all be worth it. All the years of work and sacrifice, the hours and hours of practice, the falls, the aches, the pressure, the loneliness. . . .

"Ouch."

The pain in Lisa's left ankle snapped her out of her early morning fantasy. It was six A.M. and the air was damp and cold. Lisa wasn't in the skating rink at Lake Placid or Sarajevo. She was

2

in the run-down Capitol Ice Rink in Rose Hill, Maryland. Instead of a sequined skating dress, she wore gray sweat pants, an old wool turtleneck, and a mismatched pair of gloves—one blue and one green. Lisa wasn't sharing the rink with the best of international competition but with two other local skaters, both of them trying to skate and wake up at the same time. And instead of flag-waving crowds, there was only one person up in the bleachers — Lisa's mother, who sat patiently knitting.

Lisa reached down and rubbed her ankle.

"Come on, feet," she said softly. "I know it's no fun, but go to it anyway."

It had to be done. Morning practice had nothing to do with the glamorous whirls and leaps of figure skating. From six to nine A.M. Lisa rented her "patch" of ice and worked on figures. Over and over she slowly traced one of the many versions of the figure eight until the drawings covered her section of the rink. This was the most exacting, tedious part of being a skater. Although Lisa was good at figures, it was still a chore.

Lisa breathed in the familiar rink smell — a combination of chemicals, wood, and wet wool. Pushing a few strands of dark hair out of her eyes, she tried to visualize the figure that she was going to skate. She was about to trace a forward outside eight, a very basic exercise. Gliding slowly on one foot, Lisa began her figure, remembering to control the edge of her skate and move at a steady rate. She leaned into the curve and changed feet when she came to the intersection of the second circle. Keeping her hips steady and her arms out

3

for balance, she retraced the figure three times.

With a little sigh, Lisa finished her figure and stepped away to check the accuracy of her tracing. She had done well — the circles were even, and her three tracings consistent enough to look like one line. Still, the more Lisa looked at her two perfect circles, the more listless she felt.

Lately she had been feeling as though she were inside one of those circles and she couldn't get out. It was as if everyone else was on the outside and she couldn't reach them, she couldn't step over the line to get to them. When Lisa got that feeling, she would slip into a fantasy of how she wished things would be. Like this morning. In her dream she would win, her friends would share her victory, her parents would be proud. But most of all, she would feel full and happy. Part of the world. Not lonely anymore.

Lisa looked up to see Rick Gillam, one of her fellow skaters, gliding up to her. He skated easily along the outside edge of the ice, careful not to disturb her patch.

"Hey, Lis, Shelley found out about a great new ballet class in D.C. somewhere. You should ask her about it."

"Thanks, I will," Lisa answered and watched him skate over to Shelley Baird, the third skater in the rink. Rick kissed Shelley on the mouth before going back to his own training.

Lisa had once dated Rick, before he and Shelley had become close. Lisa had met Rick when Mr. Helde had suggested they try working together as a team for pairs skating. The chemistry hadn't worked on the ice. That hadn't sur-

4

prised Lisa. The chemistry hadn't worked off the ice either.

And yet it worried Lisa that things had not worked out for them. All the skaters she knew dated other skaters. Rick was nice-looking, bright, and certainly shared her interests. But all he talked about was skating, so it was like being inside one of those circles again. Rick had made the circle even more claustrophobic. Still, Lisa couldn't help wondering. If she couldn't fall in love with Rick, maybe she couldn't fall in love with anybody.

Lisa tried to start another figure, but her mind continued to wander. Now she was daydreaming about what it would be like to do things that other sixteen-year-old girls did. To go to dances, parties, to enjoy her old friends, all the things that skating had eliminated from her life and most kids her age took for granted. She wondered what it would be like to really be part of Chris and Phoebe's crowd, the group that certainly would have been important in her life if she had not been a skater.

She looked up into the bleachers and saw her mother put down her knitting and slide over to make room for Mr. Helde, who was not only Lisa's teacher but the owner of the rink. The old man was talking animatedly to Mrs. Chang as they watched her. They were discussing her again. This was the third morning in a row, and Lisa was starting to get very curious. She saw Mr. Helde nod his head and stand up, then both he and her mother began to walk down the bleachers toward the ice.

Lisa suddenly felt nervous. She flipped her shoulder-length black hair away from her face and slowly peeled off her gloves. Her mother acknowledged Lisa's expectant look and answered it with a reassuring smile. Her mother's wide face and almond-shaped eyes seemed to hold some kind of secret.

"Lisa."

"Yeah, Mom."

"Why don't you take a break and join us in the snack shop?"

"Okay."

Lisa's mother and Mr. Helde headed for the refreshment area. Feeling a tinge of apprehension, Lisa hopped off the ice and onto the rubber matting. In one motion she wiped the moisture from her skate blades and clipped on a pair of plastic blade guards. She could see inside the snack shop through the clouded glass window. Her mother and Coach Helde were still talking.

Lisa walked into the shop and was immediately presented with a styrofoam cup of Mr. Helde's special brand of Swiss cocoa.

"How's your ankle?" Lisa's mom asked as soon as Lisa sat down. She blew on her coffee to cool it off.

"I only feel it if I'm a little stiff or tired. It's almost better." Lisa had injured her ankle in a fall the previous month. It seemed it was taking forever to totally heal.

"Do you feel that you're at your best right now or do you need more time for it to mend?" Mr. Helde asked seriously. He had a thick European

6

accent and a gray mustache that he wiped with a paper napkin after each sip of coffee.

"It doesn't bother me too much," Lisa said, trying to sound casual. She looked from her mother to her old teacher. They both looked so intent: her mom's dark eyes full of concern, Mr. Helde's craggy face creased with worry.

"So what's up?" Lisa asked. She was not one for suspense. If something was going on and it concerned her, she wanted to know what it was.

Mr. Helde drained his cup. Finally, after a pause that took forever, he began. "Coach Bielman, from the sports center in Colorado, he is coming east next week. He would like to have another look at you."

Lisa slowly put down her cocoa and swallowed hard. Bielman was the most famous figure-skating coach in the country. He had coached almost every American medal-winner in the last two Olympics. He made the difference between a talented skater and a champion. Last year at the Eastern division competition he had watched Lisa perform. His judgment was that her athletic ability was impressive but that she didn't yet show the winner's quality he was looking for. He wanted skaters who could do more than just execute the difficult moves. He was looking for skaters who projected that extra something that makes certain people stars.

"You mean he'll come here . . . to Rose Hill . . . just to see me?" Lisa asked shakily. It was an extraordinary second chance. And a scary one.

"Ya." Mr. Helde nodded. "He wants to look

7

at a boy skater in Virginia, and I've been telling him how much you are improving." Helde looked away modestly.

Of course, Lisa thought gratefully. It was Mr. Helde's doing. Her old teacher had probably been badgering Bielman since he had turned her down a year ago.

"Lisa, it's a wonderful opportunity," Mrs. Chang put in, "but, of course, it's up to you. Would you like to skate for Coach Bielman again?"

Lisa knew that it was not a simple question. Of course she wanted another chance to work with the greatest of all skating teachers. And yet despite Mr. Helde's praise, she was not feeling any better about her skating than she had the last time Coach Bielman had seen her. If anything, she was feeling worse.

But Lisa also knew that this would probably be her last opportunity to make the move toward a possible Olympic career. A sixteen-year-old figure skater was not considered young. Looking over at Mr. Helde's tired face, Lisa thought about the years of support and guidance he had given her. She and her old teacher had enormous affection for each other, yet they both knew that Lisa had outgrown his coaching. The only way for her to really become a first-class skater was for Bielman to take her.

"Yes. I want to skate for Coach Bielman," Lisa said firmly. Her mother had often said there was no point in doing something if you were only going to do it halfway. Lisa knew that was true.

"You're prepared to move to Colorado if he

decides he wants you?" Mr. Helde leaned in to ask. "You would move away from your friends, your school . . . even your family if Bielman says yes?"

Lisa looked at her mother, who gave her a supportive nod. They had talked about this before.

"Yes," Lisa said, clutching her cup a little too tightly, "to work with Coach Bielman I would even be willing to leave my life in Rose Hill and move to Colorado."

Her voice shook a little as she said it, and Lisa hoped that it was true.

Chapter
2

"Hey, Cardinals, that was Kenny Graystoke and the Longines, a new group out of New York City. From what I just heard, they're no threat to The Jacksons, and probably not to anyone else either."

Peter Lacey sat at his control board and smiled to himself. It was his favorite time of the day — his noontime radio show. Sometimes he wondered how he'd ever managed to get to be the Kennedy High DJ for WKND, the school station. He knew he was good at it, and he worked incredibly hard to keep the station going. It was just that he had such a great time as DJ that he couldn't imagine why every other Kennedy student didn't want the job, too.

"And now," announced Peter, "on to something a little better. This one is my personal favorite. You all know who I mean. The boss, Bruce Springsteen! You guess the name of the song. It's been number one here for the last week."

Peter switched off the microphone, cued the turntable, and brought up the volume. He stood up and began to move to the music, the shirttails of his antique-yellow bowling shirt coming untucked from his well-worn jeans. Bruce Springsteen's rock and roll was doing its thing out over the Kennedy campus. It came as a joyful explosion for Peter, who followed the music with his feet, his hips, his hands.

Peter loved spending his lunchtimes in the small, windowless studio of WKND. Even when the skies were sunny and clear and he knew that the rest of his crowd was enjoying the good weather outside in the Kennedy quad, he didn't care. There was nowhere he liked better than the radio station. Sometimes he felt like it was the greatest toy a seventeen-year-old boy could ever have.

There was a knock at the control booth door. "Come in," Peter called, without missing a beat.

"Hi, Peter."

It was his station assistant, Janie Barstow. She was loaded down with a stack of albums, and there was a timid smile on her plain, slender face. Always so sweet and dependable, Janie was one of the people who made Peter's show possible. Janie did the "scut" work. She filed records, brought sandwiches, cleaned up, kept track of requests — all the stuff that was absolutely essential if WKND was going to stay on the air. Janie had even taken a crack at soldering speaker wires.

"Janie!" Peter mouthed, although his words were barely audible above the music, "good to see you!" Then, still dancing, Peter relieved Janie of the albums and tried to get her to join his uninhibited two-step. Too shy to respond, Janie blushed and pulled two neatly wrapped sandwiches from the book bag that hung over her shoulder.

Peter reached up and tousled Janie's fine brown hair. Since she was a few inches taller than Peter, he had to stand on his tiptoes to do it. But it was Peter's favorite way to greet his friend. He took the wrapped sandwiches, made a gesture of eternal thanks, and began to gobble the first one down.

At the end of the record — and Peter's first sandwich — he motioned for Janie to be quiet. Bringing up the microphone, Peter casually announced the next cut. As soon as the music started up, Peter flipped off the main studio speaker so that he and his radio partner could talk.

"Hey, Janie," Peter exclaimed, "did you hear that first record I played today? What a piece of noise. I couldn't believe it. I thought I was at the dentist's office."

Janie laughed again, this time bending over slightly so that her long, limp hair dangled in her face.

"I mean, where'd we get a record that bad?" Peter joked.

"I think it was something one of the record companies sent us as a promotion," Janie said in her soft voice.

"Bad," Peter remarked, "and not good bad like Tina Turner. Bad bad like something that hurts your ears." Peter pushed a lock of wavy brown hair out of his eyes and smiled good-naturedly. Janie looked down at the ground and stuck her hands in the pockets of her baggy beige skirt.

"Anyway, thanks for the lunch," Peter went on. "You're the original Kennedy lifesaver, Miss Barstow." Peter put out a hand to Janie and touched her arm.

It wasn't much of a touch, but it felt like a jolt of electricity to Janie. She started to giggle again and hoped that Peter wasn't wondering why. She was relieved to see that all Peter's attention was now on his digital watch, which he was synchronizing with the old clock on the wall. With a blush, Janie wondered if Peter had any idea how she really felt about him. She hoped not. She hoped he never would find out.

"So, anyway," Peter said, "we've got to play some decent tunes for at least the next ten minutes until you-know-who gets here."

Janie nodded. You-know-who was Laurie Bennington, the social activities officer for the student council. Laurie was gorgeous, perfectly dressed, and she scared the heck out of Janie. Twice a week Laurie came on the radio show to announce the schedule of upcoming Kennedy events.

"Janie," Peter said seriously, "can I ask you something?"

Janie stood up straighter and pushed her bangs away from her eyes. "Of course," she peeped.

Peter slowly unwrapped the second sandwich.

"What do you think of what Laurie is doing on this station?"

"What do you mean?" asked Janie. Janie wanted to say something more profound and tell Peter exactly what it was he needed to know, but she really didn't know what to say. Just being in the same room with him never failed to leave her tongue-tied.

"I mean, she was supposed to be announcing all the upcoming stuff for the student council. That's okay. But from the first time she's come on, all she's done is use the show as her own private gossip program. Man, it bugs me."

Before Janie could answer, Peter held up a finger for her to wait and quickly faded out one record while cueing up another.

"Well," Janie began hesitantly, after Peter brought up the sound on the second turntable, "I know that the two of you don't get along very well. . . ."

Peter started to laugh, as if Janie had just made the understatement of the century.

"But she's so popular," Janie insisted, "a lot of kids love her show." Janie looked at Peter with her wide brown eyes and hoped he wouldn't mind her telling him something he probably didn't want to hear.

"I know you're right. It just drives me wacko. Anybody on Laurie's dog list gets a public put-down over the radio. She's really into ruining reputations. And that's not what this radio station is for."

Janie nodded in agreement. In spite of Peter's

cool exterior, he was truly fair and caring. That was one of the things that made him so easy to fall for.

"Ah," Peter continued disgustedly, "maybe she just does it to drive me crazy." He began to drum on the control panel with a pencil.

"Why would Laurie do that?"

Peter swerved in his chair and checked the record. He still had a minute or so left. He spun back to face Janie.

"It's ridiculous. I guess Bennington liked me for a while, and I wasn't interested, so she's been on the warpath ever since. Anytime she can do anything to bug me, it makes her super happy."

Peter shrugged his shoulders and continued. "I can't wait to see what she pulls with these homecoming princess interviews. You know I'm supposed to interview all the candidates on the show. I mean, usually I love doing stuff like that, it's just that Bennington is in charge."

Peter gave Janie another shush sign as he smoothly swung the dangling microphone in front of him and flipped back the toggle switch.

"How'd you like that one, Cardinals? WKND can still give you a little kick over the airwaves. Speaking of kicks, I was just talking with my friendly station organizer here — the person who really keeps this show going, Janie Barstow — and we were just discussing what's coming up this week. Everybody out there must know that homecoming is not far off — the big game, the big dance, and the nomination and selection of candidates for queen and princess.

"WKND is going to be keeping you up on all of that, right here. This week I'm going to begin interviewing the charming, beautiful ladies who will be your candidates for the honor of princess. You're not going to want to miss that. Now, in the meantime, for all you fans of that new sultry songstress from San Francisco, Joan Stuart Morris. . . ."

Peter talked on, but Janie could think only about homecoming. It was one of the biggest dances of the year, but like almost every dance, Janie wouldn't get to go. Nobody would think of asking her. Peter turned off the microphone and looked at Janie. "So, you going to be around this week to help me with the interviews?"

Janie nodded and opened the door to let some air into the stuffy studio.

Peter smiled. "That's great. I'm really going to need your help."

"Peter," Janie asked in a nervous whisper, "are you taking anybody to the homecoming dance?" She tried to make it sound casual. She knew it really wasn't her business, but she just had to know.

"Nah. I'm just going to wing it. I don't want to get caught up in that corsage, wearing-a-suit weirdness," Peter answered.

Janie smiled shyly. She knew that Peter had never had a steady girl friend, even though girls were always throwing themselves at him. She had seen it often enough at the station. Peter would pay ten times more attention to WKND than he did to the girl, and she would quickly give up. When Peter did talk about going out, he usually

16

meant with his whole crowd. Formal dates were not Peter's style.

"I'm gonna go . . . you know," Peter continued, "just to play records between sets. They've got some group from D.C. playing. I've never heard of them myself, but Laurie dug them out of some —"

"Well, then maybe I should go, too, and help you with the records. I mean, setting everything up and all that. I mean if that's okay?" Janie interrupted.

Peter grinned. "Okay . . ." he said enthusiastically. "Hey, sure! I can always use your help."

Janie would have liked to lean over the turntables and give Peter a huge hug. That is, if she had had the nerve to do something like that. She knew that it was hardly a date, but just going to the dance and helping Peter with the records would be one of the best times that she could imagine. She broke into a huge smile.

"Oh, Peter, you know what I heard," Janie bubbled, finally inspired that she had something to contribute.

"What?"

"Well, the girls in gym were talking about Laurie and Brenda Austin. You know, Chris Austin's stepsister?"

Peter nodded. Chris was a good friend of his. Brenda was Chris's dark-haired stepsister who had transferred to Kennedy a year ago after her mother had married Chris's father.

"So," Janie continued, "Brenda told one girl in our gym class that she ran into Laurie Bennington in Georgetown and Laurie was buying this incredibly expensive suit for homecoming. And, according to Brenda, Laurie doesn't even have a date!"

Janie gave a little giggle, knowing that she really shouldn't spread gossip, but feeling sure that Peter would enjoy any disparaging news about Laurie. From the amused look on Peter's face, Janie knew that her tidbit had been appreciated.

Suddenly Janie's giggling came to an abrupt halt, and she felt her face grow flushed with humiliation. Laurie Bennington was standing in the doorway and had obviously just overheard what Janie had said.

"Interesting what comes out of Brenda Austin's mouth," Laurie mocked in a voice that was like barbed wire. She stood in the doorway with her hand resting on the edge of the heavy door. Her hair was short and hennaed and fell sexily over one eye. She wore a short leather skirt, cherry-red sweater, and cream-colored high-heeled boots.

"Well, Janie, dear," Laurie went on, "maybe I don't have a date — yet. But sometimes you have to take a chance and wait for the one you really want. You, of all people, know about that, right?" She cast an obvious glance over at Peter, and then back at Janie.

Janie felt a surge of embarrassment. Did Laurie know about the terrible crush she had on Peter? No . . . please, no. Even worse, had Peter picked up on Laurie's blatant hint? With relief, Janie saw that Peter was totally involved in timing his last record of the day. He didn't seem to have noticed anything.

"You have to watch who you listen to," Laurie added coldly.

Janie didn't know how to respond. If there was anybody who could make her feel like a useless, plain, dumb, unpopular nothing, it was Laurie Bennington.

"And another thing," Laurie said archly, "I think you have better things to worry about than me finding a date for homecoming."

Janie nodded quietly and looked away from Laurie. *Why did I ever say anything about Laurie Bennington?* she thought to herself. It was one of those moments when she wished she could sink right through the floor.

Chapter 3

"Well, honey, it's set. Coach Bielman is coming to see you next Monday."

Lisa felt her shoulders tense and her heart beat a little bit faster. Looking out the car window, she watched the familiar colonial-style shops and restaurants of downtown Rose Hill glide by as her mom drove her to school.

It was a brisk November day, and the leaves along the roadside were fading. Not much bright yellow and orange left; now the streets were brown and gray, the trees turning to skeletons as the sky began to cloud over. Her mom's words made Lisa feel edgy and scared, and the weather did little to help.

"He probably won't take me," Lisa mumbled as she zipped up the jacket of her lavender sweat suit.

She had said it so quickly that her mother probably hadn't heard. That was okay. Lisa wasn't even sure she wanted to talk about it. Instead, she pulled down the sun visor of her mom's old Chevrolet and looked in the mirror. She began to take out the hairpins that had held up her hair during her morning practice. Now her hair fell like a straight black curtain around her face. If Bielman did take her, he would probably make her cut her hair very short like most other skaters. She didn't really want that. Trying to imagine what she would look like with short, cropped hair, Lisa made a face and decided it would not be an improvement.

She was wearing no makeup and looked a bit pale, her dark eyes a little tired. She pinched her cheeks to give her face some color. Then she began searching for her mascara, but she couldn't find it in her messy bag. Ace bandage, leg warmers, gloves, skate laces — there were plenty of those. But a simple tube of mascara . . . no. It was like her closet at home. Tights, sweat suits, leotards, and skating skirts of every color and cut. And yet when she had to go anywhere outside the rink, there was never anything to wear.

"Coach Bielman may want you or he may not." Mrs. Chang stopped at a red light and turned to her daughter. "Whatever happens, you know you have our support. As long as you try your best, that's all we want." She brushed the side of Lisa's hair back behind her ear.

So her mom had heard her. Of course she had.

"I know, Mom," Lisa returned. Her parents had made almost as many sacrifices for her skating career as she had. They had big hopes. Lisa didn't want to disappoint them.

21

"Have you thought any more about what it would really be like to leave Rose Hill and move by yourself to Colorado?" Mrs. Chang pulled into the intersection and made a left turn. "What about your friends?"

Lisa gave a tiny frown. Her friends! Between leaving school every day at noon and spending all her free time at the rink or in dance class, Lisa never saw the few friends she did have. Like Phoebe Hall. When Lisa was younger — when she spent only two hours a day at the rink — she and Phoebe had been very good friends. But Lisa could remember exactly when that friendship had started to fade.

It had been the slumber party for Phoebe's fourteenth birthday. Lisa hadn't slept over because she had an important qualifying test at the rink the next day, and her mom didn't think she'd get enough sleep at the party. So Lisa had left after Phoebe had opened her presents. The rest of the girls stayed up all night and had a séance, told each other's fortunes, even used Sasha Jenkins's Ouija board. Come Monday morning they were all talking about how they had communicated with spirits and lifted Phoebe off the ground almost without touching her. They had all shared something in the late hours of the night that bound them together and left Lisa out.

"You know, Mom, I hardly ever see my friends anymore," Lisa said, staring out the window. "But when I do see them, it's like we're from different planets. They're all involved in dances and football games and school stuff, and I barely know what they're talking about." Lisa thought

22

about the times she rode by the school after a late jazz class and saw all the kids pouring excitedly into the football stadium. Just once she wanted to run in and join them.

"Every worthwhile thing demands certain sacrifices," Mrs. Chang said sweetly and patted Lisa on the arm.

Lisa knew her mom was right, that you couldn't have everything. Lisa also knew that she was incredibly lucky to have the ability and the support to do something like figure skating. Still, sometimes she couldn't help wondering if what she had sacrificed wasn't more important than what she was achieving. Being a good athlete was great, but not at the expense of being a full human being.

As if Lisa's mom had read her mind, she added, "I know it's hard sometimes now, but you'll be very glad when you're older that you never gave up."

When you're older, thought Lisa, *when Coach Bielman takes you . . . when you win a national championship . . . when you compete in the Olympics. All that was fine, but what about right now!*

Mrs. Chang made a quick right turn and followed a school bus for a few blocks until they came to the entrance to Kennedy High School. The parking lot spread out before them as a line of cars pulled in. The school stretched back behind it, a maze of low, modern buildings edged by a large athletic field. The flag was flapping in the breeze, and Lisa's fellow students were busily chatting while crowding around outside waiting

23

for friends and the first bell. At last Mrs. Chang pulled up in front of the main entrance and Lisa began to gather her books and jam them into her canvas book bag.

Just before she opened the car door, she heard a tapping on the window and looked up to see a gorgeous girl with stylishly short hair. She was wearing a black jump suit that showed off every curve of her splendid figure. Lisa rolled down the window, but she wasn't sure who the girl was.

"Hi, Lisa! I'm so glad I found you. I've been waiting all morning!" The girl sounded very excited.

Then it came to Lisa. The girl was Laurie Bennington. Lisa remembered Phoebe and Chris talking once about how Laurie had moved to Rose Hill the summer before. Lisa didn't know much else about her.

"Hi," Lisa answered curiously. She introduced Laurie to her mother.

"It's an honor to meet you, Mrs. Chang. You must be very proud to have such a gifted daughter," Laurie gushed in an overly sweet voice. Mrs. Chang nodded and thanked her.

"I'm so glad I caught you," Laurie went on. "I have something very important to tell you."

"What's that?" Lisa asked simply.

"Well, I don't know if you know about this, but I'm the new social activities officer on the student council."

Lisa nodded. She vaguely remembered hearing that Laurie was at the center of what went on at Kennedy, but she was never very up on things like that.

24

"And, of course, homecoming is very soon."
Laurie paused to see Lisa's reaction.

Lisa smiled uneasily. She had no idea that
homecoming was coming up. She was a little embarrassed that she was so unaware of one of the
most important events of the school year.

"And, we're in the process of nominating girls
for homecoming queen and princesses, and . . .
well, I get to nominate a girl for junior princess
and . . ." Laurie paused and grinned with excitement.

"Yes?"

"I've decided to nominate you!"

Lisa's mouth fell open. "Me?"

"Yes, you!"

Lisa just sat there. She wasn't sure what to
think. It was flattering that someone wanted her
to run and considered her important enough to
nominate. And she wanted to be a part of Kennedy High. Just once. Still, Lisa had the feeling
that there was something not right about her
running for homecoming princess. Laurie was
smiling at her eagerly.

"But, Laurie, I'm not involved in anything at
school. I haven't done anything for Kennedy.
You know what I mean." Lisa looked up out of
the window.

Laurie crouched down alongside the car and
rested her elbows in the window frame. She gave
Mrs. Chang a bright smile and leaned forward.
"Look, by being such a great athlete you have
given the junior class incredible honor and pres-
tige. If that isn't doing something for your school,
I don't know what is. Besides, you're a good stu-

dent, great-looking, and everybody adores you. Who would be a better candidate?"

Lisa was starting to get embarrassed by Laurie's flattery. "But, Laurie, wouldn't I have to, I don't know, campaign or go to events or things like that? I have to be at the rink five hours a day, plus all my dance classes. . . ."

"No problem," Laurie burst in as if she'd thought all this out beforehand. "All you'll have to do is go to the dance, which will be really fun, and give one interview over the school radio station at lunch hour."

With a look at her mom, Lisa wondered what to do. She wanted to be part of something at school, especially if she did end up going away to Colorado. She should have something to remember of her life in Rose Hill. Even though Lisa sensed that there was something odd about Laurie's announcement, she wanted to say yes. "Mom, it wouldn't interfere with training."

Mrs. Chang smiled. "I think it would be a good idea. It will be nice for you to do something with your old friends, something with school. As far as the radio interview goes, you could use the experience."

But suddenly Lisa felt her excitement fall away. She thought about the dance — she didn't have a date. How could she go to the homecoming dance without a date? In an embarrassed mumble, she explained her problem to Laurie.

Laurie smiled reassuringly. "Don't worry. I'll take care of that. I'll find someone very nice to be your escort, and you won't have to worry about

26

a thing. I promise you'll have a great time. Well? Will you accept the nomination?"

Lisa still had a funny feeling about the whole thing, but the more she thought about it the more she really wanted to go. "Yeah. I mean, sure, I accept. Thanks."

Laurie clapped her hands together and gave Lisa a little hug through the car window.

"Thanks, Laurie," Lisa responded. "It was really good of you to think of me."

Laurie gave a little toss of her hennaed head. "I know" — she laughed — "believe me, I know."

Chapter
4

Phoebe Hall and Chris Austin hovered around Chris's kitchen table and stared at a brown lump of dough that sat pathetically in a large wooden bowl.

"Are you sure this is right?" Phoebe asked, pushing her thick red hair with a floury hand. "It looks like you could use it for acts of terrorism."

Chris laughed and poked the heavy, dark dough with her index finger. "I should have known better than to listen to Sasha. I think she would rather die than use white flour for anything." Chris bent down and pulled a pizza pan from a low cabinet. Her long blonde hair was swept up in a French braid, which fell against her striped Oxford-cloth shirt.

"It didn't rise at all, Chris. Do you think we should still try to roll it out?" Phoebe grabbed the rolling pin and tried not to get flour all over the front of her pink overalls.

Chris looked up at the clock on the spotless kitchen wall. "Brenda and my stepmom are going to be home in half an hour. I said I'd make dinner. We might as well give it a try. At least my dad won't be home."

Phoebe nodded. Chris's father did tend to be a bit particular about things. But Chris didn't seem to worry about pleasing him quite as much as she used to. Chris had learned a lot in the last month, including not to worry so much about what other people expected of her.

"How are things going with Brenda?" Phoebe asked as she let the lump of dough fall onto the floured board. It landed with a dull thud. "Maybe we should just put this dough out of its misery."

Chris rolled her eyes as she went over to the pan of sauce that was simmering on the stove. "Things with Brenda are a little better," she answered, referring to her stepsister. She stuck her finger in the sauce and tasted it. "Mmm."

"Hey, maybe we should just serve the sauce in bowls, like soup." Phoebe tried to roll out the dough but quickly resorted to pounding it out with her fists. "Did you put wheat germ or something in here, too?"

"And bran," Chris admitted sheepishly. "Sasha said to." They both laughed. Sasha was a friend of theirs who was famous for her contributions to the school newspaper and her health-food diet.

"I'm lucky I can lift it," Phoebe cracked. "You know, I saw Brenda at school today and she actually said hi to me. I think she even smiled. Maybe."

Chris took a large hunk of cheese from the refrigerator and started to grate it. "Ever since the night of Laurie Bennington's party, Brenda and I have been getting along better. She's still distant sometimes, but we can at least talk now."

"That's good." Phoebe still had a hard time picturing Chris and Brenda as pals. Even though they were stepsisters, the two girls were as different in personality as they were in appearance. Chris was a terrific student with all-American blond good looks, who always strove to keep the highest standards. Brenda was dusky and dark, with a mysterious rebelliousness that had once led to her running away from home. That had been over a year ago, but since that time and until very recently, Brenda and Chris had barely been able to speak to each other.

Maybe Laurie's party had actually helped to make things better between the two stepsisters. At least some good had come out of that party. Phoebe still had a hard time thinking back on that night without shuddering. At the time it had all been so painful.

That night had been the end of Phoebe's relationship with Brad, the boy she'd dated for so long. Chris and her boyfriend Ted had broken up the week before and were still stumbling around like the walking wounded. Finally, straight arrow Chris had gotten so upset that she tried to ease her pain with a large dose of vodka. Taking a misstep like that — especially for the girl who never allowed herself to make mistakes — was a big lesson.

Chris had taken her lesson to heart. She was now softer, more tolerant of others and herself. Ted was back in Chris's life, and Phoebe felt her friend was more open and generous. That things were better with Brenda was another sign of how Chris had changed.

"Hey, Chris," Phoebe said softly. She craned her neck to look out the front window and make sure that Mrs. Austin and Brenda were nowhere in sight. "Did Brenda ever tell your parents about your getting drunk at Laurie's party?"

Chris made a face at the mention of that most embarrassing incident. She had not only broken up with Ted, but she had also had a terrible fight with Phoebe. And there she had been, sitting all alone in the backyard at Laurie's party. She'd found that bottle of vodka and proceeded to get very drunk. It was such an un-Chris-like thing to do that it was hard to believe it had really happened. Luckily, with the exception of Laurie and Brenda, no one but a few close friends knew about it.

"You know, Pheeb, Brenda never did tell on me. Even after all this time, with her being the one who's always in trouble and me being the goody-goody. She had her chance to prove that I could mess up, too, and she didn't do it."

"Wow."

"Yeah. I really respect her for that. I hope I can do the same kind of thing for her sometime."

Phoebe went back to pounding out the brown

31

pizza dough and measured it against the large pan. "I'd try and spin this like they do at the pizza shop, but I'm afraid I'd smash a hole in your ceiling."

"Not a good idea," agreed Chris.

"No."

Phoebe managed to lay the thick crust over the pan. There was a short lull in the conversation. Finally she took a deep breath and spoke in a very cautious voice. "Chris, do you know that Laurie Bennington is spreading some ugly gossip about Brenda?"

Chris stopped grating and looked at Phoebe with her very blue eyes. "I know. I've been trying to ignore those remarks she keeps making on her radio show. She's being just as nasty about me."

"Well, we both know why." Phoebe shook her head. It was very obvious that Laurie was mad because of Peter Lacey. All of Laurie's designs on Peter had been rendered useless when Peter had left her party early to help take care of Chris.

"Yeah." Chris nodded. "I've gone over it in my mind. It's so dumb that Laurie thinks I ruined her big chance with Peter. She thinks that if Peter hadn't helped take me home, he would have fallen into her arms."

"I know."

"I still can't believe she doesn't just face the fact that he never liked her in the first place." Chris spread sauce over the pizza crust and swooshed it around with a big wooden spoon.

"As we've both come to realize, Laurie Bennington is not what you would call a logical, fair-minded person. I just wish we'd both seen through

32

her earlier. Now she's out to get you, and Brenda, and Peter and probably half the Kennedy student body. I'll tell you, I can't imagine Laurie and Peter together in that little radio station room."

"Nuclear fission, if you ask me."

Phoebe pushed up the sleeves of her white sweat shirt. "I guess you'd better be prepared to deal with her when you run for homecoming princess."

Chris tossed the spoon into the sink and looked at Phoebe with a stunned smile. "What makes you think I'll even be nominated for homecoming princess."

"Oh, come on, Chris," Phoebe teased as she swatted her best friend on the rear end. "You're only smart and popular, not to mention the girl friend of the star quarterback. Must I go on?"

Chris blushed and waved her hand in a gesture of disbelief.

"I mean, you can never be sure who will win the crown," continued Phoebe, "but I can't even imagine that you won't at least be nominated."

"Well, we'll see," Chris answered primly. "In the meantime I'm sure Laurie will do whatever she can to stop me. I just hope she doesn't take it out on Brenda. I won't put up with that." She sprinkled the grated cheese on the pizza, then stepped back to look at her creation.

Both girls began to giggle. It looked pretty awful. But Phoebe told Chris it wasn't a total failure because at least it made both of them laugh. Phoebe hadn't been doing enough of that lately. This was the first afternoon in nearly a month when her spirits had been high. Though when she started to think about the homecoming dance, she could feel her mood start to sag again.

It was just that Phoebe had spent every homecoming since she'd been at Kennedy with her ex-boyfriend, Brad Davidson. Now that they had broken up, it was weird to think about homecoming without him.

"What is it, Pheeb?" Chris asked sweetly. She untied the terry cloth apron from around her denim skirt and hung it in the narrow broom closet.

"Oh, I was just thinking about Brad. He won't even look me in the eye now. It's like he can't stand to be in the same room with me."

Chris stacked the dishes in the sink and began to wash them. "I guess I know how he feels. When Ted and I were split up, I pretended that I never wanted to see him. But the truth was that I was thinking about him all the time and secretly hoping I'd run into him or hear from him. Eventually I guess I got it through my thick skull that we should make up."

Phoebe smiled. It was nice that Ted and Chris had found each other again. They belonged together. But she and Brad were a different story. Phoebe felt deep down that breaking up with Brad *was* the right thing to do. Even though it was so hard.

"Pheeb," Chris said thoughtfully, "I think it's just that Brad still loves you and it hurts too much for him to see you."

Phoebe looked down at her floury hands and sighed.

"While we're on the subject," Chris said matter-of-factly, "anything new with Griffin?"

Phoebe felt her heart give a tug inside. She had been wanting to talk about Griffin all afternoon, but she was trying to control it. It seemed as if every time she'd seen Chris recently she'd rambled on about Griffin.

Griffin had been one big reason for the end of her relationship with Brad. He had been like no one Phoebe had ever known: bold, spirited, always confident, incredibly imaginative.

But they'd had so little time together. Phoebe understood how much Griffin wanted to be an actor, and that he'd had to grab his chance to audition for a play in New York. And Phoebe knew that Griffin never did anything halfway. That was why he'd made the move away from Rose Hill and quit Kennedy High to live in New York City. Still, understanding all that didn't make the separation any easier.

Phoebe motioned for Chris to come back over to the table and to keep her voice down. Finally Phoebe told her friend the latest.

"Griffin called me last night," Phoebe whispered. She couldn't help the grin that covered her face as she talked about Griffin.

"Really, when?"

"Late. So late, in fact, I think my parents would have killed me if they'd known, but they were asleep and luckily I heard the phone first. He's having a great time. He had another audition for that Broadway show. You know, the one that the agent first called him about."

Chris nodded. Griffin had come very close to getting the lead in a new Broadway play but had lost it to a young movie actor. "Yes?"

"Well, now the producers are interested in having Griffin as the understudy. He has his third call-back tomorrow, and his agent told him he'll probably get it. Isn't that great? Griffin says if he's the understudy for a while, there's a good chance the movie actor will leave to make another movie and then he'll get to take over. I can't believe it." Phoebe was grinning, but her eyes managed to well up with tears at the same time.

"You really miss him, don't you?" Chris patted her friend's hand.

"Yeah," Phoebe admitted quietly, "I really miss him."

Just at that moment they heard a car pull into the driveway. Chris gave Phoebe's forearm a light squeeze before going to the hall and opening the front door.

It was Catherine — Chris's stepmother — and Brenda. The two of them had been to the dentist, and Brenda was tenderly touching her lower lip as she walked in the front door.

"Hi," said Brenda with a slight smile. Her layered dark hair waved down to her shoulders, and she was wearing a black sweater vest and tight blue jeans. "I'm numb," she mumbled, continuing to poke her mouth as she walked into the kitchen.

Catherine followed soon after and gave Chris a peck on the cheek as she wandered through the kitchen and on out into the dining room. Brenda stopped at the kitchen table and stared at the pizza with a puzzled face.

"If no one breaks their jaws, it'll be a great dinner," Phoebe joked. Chris came over and stood next to her.

Brenda looked at Chris and Phoebe. There was an awkward silence. Brenda finally shifted her weight and said, "I knew there was a reason I asked for Novocaine."

Chris and Phoebe began to laugh. For a moment Brenda stared silently at them. Finally, her delicate face broke into a smile, and she allowed herself to laugh, too.

Chapter
5

"Chris, do you think it's still raining outside?" Phoebe looked across the crowded Kennedy lunchroom and then tugged nervously on the sleeve of Chris's blue tweed blazer. The whole business of Chris's homecoming nomination was making her feel jumpy.

"It's no big deal, Pheeb. We can listen to the radio announcement perfectly well here in the lunchroom."

It was the day that Laurie Bennington would announce the junior princess nominees over WKND. Chris was acting like none of it mattered, but Phoebe knew that she was all ears. Trouble was that it was usually so noisy in the lunchroom, it was difficult to make out what Peter or any other announcer over WKND was saying. The place was crammed with students.

Chris took a deep breath and popped off the top of her plastic container of salad. She was trying hard to act cool and composed. Not Phoebe. She stood up and stuck her hands in the pockets of her striped jeans. Balanced on tiptoes in her cowboy boots, Phoebe looked for some of their other friends.

"Look, here comes Ted. Maybe he can talk you into going out to the quad."

Chris turned around and waved at her boyfriend as he strode across the cafeteria. Ted was wearing his letterman's jacket, khaki slacks, and a faded yellow sweat shirt. His blondish hair was curly and there was a mischievous look in his blue eyes. He gracefully avoided an awkward freshman and scooted past a cafeteria worker carrying a huge plastic bag. Nimble Ted — no wonder he was the first-string quarterback on the football team. Finally he got to the table, put his lunch tray down, and made Chris scoot over to make room for him. "So when's Laurie going to announce?" he asked anxiously.

Chris playfully slapped him on the arm. "You're as bad as Phoebe. You guys all act like it's such a big deal."

Ted winked at Phoebe. "No big deal. I don't care if you get homecoming princess or not. Maybe we won't even bother to go to the dance. It's never any fun anyway," he teased. Chris leaned over and poked him in the side with her elbow. With a grin, Ted put an arm over her shoulder and pulled her back against him.

"I was just trying to talk Miss Cool-and-Composed here into going out into the quad so we can stand by one of the speakers and really hear what Laurie has to say," Phoebe told Ted.

"Sounds like a good idea to me," Ted answered. "The freshmen are always such barbarians that it's hard to have a civilized conversation in the cafeteria anyway. Let me just have a little lunch here, and then we'll go."

Chris and Phoebe looked at each other as Ted began to eat. It was amazing to them how much boys could pack away. Ted noticed and looked up at Phoebe with a what's-the-problem expression and motioned for her to hurry up. Phoebe quickly polished off her yogurt, and Chris managed to down most of her salad.

"Okay," Ted said between the last bites of his apple, "I'm ready. I can probably go another whole ten minutes without a refill."

"Gee," Chris cracked, "maybe we should have the cooks see if they can hook up some kind of intravenous line out to the quad."

Ted put up both hands in mock surrender. "I've already checked that out. A lot of advanced technology is required. They're working on it."

The three of them got up from the table. Just as they were going out, Sasha walked in. She was with another close friend, Woody Webster. Sasha was lecturing Woody, her long wavy hair swishing from side to side. Woody had his thumbs hooked in his red suspenders and was listening with an amused look on his face.

"Hey, guys," Sasha called out, "where are you going?"

"Out to the quad to hear the radio better. Wanna come?"

Sasha and Woody immediately changed direction and joined Phoebe, Chris, and Ted.

40

Sasha continued to talk to Woody. "I'm going to write an article about it for the newspaper," she emphasized. She wore an old-fashioned white cotton blouse that had lace on the collar. "See, curds and whey, like Little Miss Muffet. Well, curds are like cottage cheese, but the whey — the liquid part that we throw away — that's the part that's really good for you. In this one part of southern Russia they drink whey and they live to be one hundred and ten years old."

"Sash, I don't think I want to live to be a hundred and ten years old," Woody cracked. His dark hair was as curly as Phoebe's from the cool, damp weather, and when his redheaded friend walked alongside him he slipped his arm around her shoulder.

"Don't listen to her," Phoebe warned. "Chris and I made a pizza crust from her recipe a few days ago, and it almost broke our jaws."

Sasha smiled good-naturedly. "You're just so used to refined foods. You have to adjust to a new way of eating."

"I think I'd rather starve."

Phoebe laughed and snapped Woody's suspenders against his chest. *Good old Woody*, she thought. Woody smiled warmly at her, his soft, brown eyes twinkling.

Phoebe looked at all of them trudging out into the muddy, wet quad. Individually they were all as different as could be. Yet together they formed a well-knit unit that made each of them stronger.

Maybe that was why Phoebe loved her friends so much. Woody was goofy and funny, but also talented and original. Sasha, for all her far-out

41

ideas, was loving and loyal and great on the newspaper. Ted and Chris were playful and smart and remarkable for being content with just who they were. Peter, whose voice was beginning to come clearly through the outdoor speakers, was one of a kind. His funky style, good looks, and passion for the school radio station really set him apart. Each of them was different, but as a group they stood together and supported each other whenever they could. Phoebe didn't know what she'd do without her friends — every single one of them.

The skies were still gray, and it was drizzling. The cherry trees looked drenched and weepy, and there were puddles all over the ground. The group took shelter under the breezeway connecting the science and art classrooms. Ted pulled his collar up around his neck and put his arm protectively around Chris. There was a speaker above, and they could clearly hear Michael Jackson's high, breathy voice.

Woody began dancing, doing an accurate imitation of Michael Jackson's style, and Phoebe started giggling, but when she looked up, her laughter stopped immediately. Coming toward the group was Brad Davidson, Phoebe's ex-boyfriend. He had a big smile on his face until he saw Phoebe. Then he froze, and his smile turned into a blank stare.

The rest of the crowd saw Brad, too, and Ted started to move toward him to talk to him. But Brad made it very obvious that he didn't want to be anywhere near Phoebe. He shifted his wide shoulders and shook back his brown hair. With a stiff wave that was carefully aimed at Ted, Brad turned and walked back the other way.

For a moment everybody was silent. Phoebe felt a little sick. Why did it have to be this way? What made Brad think that they both couldn't be part of the crowd? Even with all his activities as student body president, Phoebe knew that he must miss hanging out with them. The crowd certainly missed Brad. But Phoebe also knew that it still hurt too much to have to see each other. Chris gave Phoebe a reassuring pat on the arm, but no one else said anything.

Peter's voice was coming from the overhead speaker. "Hey, Cardinals, I'm going to sign off a little early today. Guess you all know why. Today is the big day. We get to find out who will be nominated for junior homecoming princess."

Everyone looked up anxiously. Woody got so excited that he did a little dance step right into a puddle, accidentally splashing Ted and Chris.

"Nice going, Webster," Ted teased.

"Shhh, quiet!" Sasha insisted. "Listen."

"One of your favorites and mine is coming on to announce the gorgeous nominees," Peter said coolly. "Kennedy's social activities officer and a WKND regular, Laurie Bennington."

Ted hissed softly, but Chris quickly shushed him. They continued to listen.

"Hi, Peter," Laurie said with false sweetness. "I heard you ordered the rain today because you're such a big drip."

"Thanks, Laurie," Peter came back in an overly controlled tone. "That may be. But then everyone says you're all wet."

43

"Boy, those two are getting bad." Woody frowned. "I know they don't like each other, but they should try to keep it off the air."

"Knowing Laurie the way I do now, I'd say that Peter is using supreme self-control," Phoebe put in.

Laurie's voice came over the speaker again. "I know you've all been waiting out there. This is an exciting time! You heard the nominations for queen a few days ago, and the sophomore and freshman entries will come later on. But today I have the princess candidates from my very own fabulous junior class! I am going to announce them any moment. I must say I find that there is a wide selection, but I'll let you out there make the final decision."

The entire group groaned. "Nice of her to at least give us something to do," Ted remarked. Chris leaned her head against Ted's shoulder. She was trying to stay calm.

"Our first nominee is one that all Cardinals know well. That energetic beauty of a pom-pom girl, Marci Caitlin! Now, we've all seen Marci at her bubbliest out there on the football field, where she puts it on the line every week for Kennedy High. However, keep in mind that beauty is only one of the things that counts in this contest."

"Oooooo, Laurie's so nasty!" Chris grimaced. "How does she get away with it?"

"She kisses up to old Snyder, that's how," answered Woody disgustedly. "You should see it. She bats her eyes, and Snyder lets her get away with murder." Mr. Snyder was the faculty adviser for the student council, and he was a pushover when it came to gorgeous Laurie.

"The worst part is you never know when Laurie's gossip is true and when it isn't," Sasha complained. "Marci Caitlin *is* flunking half her classes."

Laurie's voice pierced the air again. "Our second nominee is that ever-responsible head of the service club. I'm speaking of none other than our own Caroline Macy! We all know how terrific Caroline has been looking recently. Hmm. Just remember that the homecoming princess has to represent us for a whole year."

"Ugh!" Woody screamed. "Caroline only just managed the near impossible feat of losing thirty pounds, and Laurie acts like she's going to gain it all back tomorrow!"

Laurie went on to briefly mention a few other names. Chris nervously chewed on her index finger.

"The next nominee is a girl many of you know as head of the Honor Society and girl friend of our illustrious quarterback."

They all sat up. Ted clapped his hands together, but Phoebe quickly gestured for quiet. She knew Laurie would have more to say.

"Of course I mean that cool blonde, Chris Austin."

Woody gave a muted hoot of approval.

"We all know what an achiever Chris is, and she's so outgoing. Chris has even been trying to bring the newest member of her family into the

Kennedy social scene. Well, from what I've heard, there's beginning to be a strong family resemblance."

"Ooo!" Chris yelled out, waving a fist at the speaker. She'd been afraid that Laurie would drag Brenda into this. Of course Laurie was referring to Chris's slipup at her party and the fact that Brenda had been in trouble. She hoped most kids wouldn't understand the veiled reference, and even Laurie wouldn't dare be more specific.

"Don't worry, Chris," Ted counseled. "Nobody takes Laurie that seriously."

Everyone nodded. They knew that Ted was right. Chris was a good candidate no matter what Laurie said.

"Now for the last nominee. First, though, you all know how I like to kid and joke. I hope no one takes my little digs seriously because I'm just trying to be entertaining. It's never the intention of my show to hurt anyone's feelings."

"Sure," Phoebe muttered.

"But I must tell you, as far as this last nominee goes, I couldn't even think of anything negative to joke about. This girl is so gifted, so intelligent, so beautiful and special that I have found it impossible to do anything but list her wonderful qualities."

"Oh, no," Woody groaned, "she's going to nominate herself."

"Some of you may know this famous girl only by reputation, but we'll make sure that you find out more about her as homecoming approaches," Laurie gushed. "Believe me, I can't think of anyone else who would represent the junior class

46

better than the one girl who might soon be a national heroine. Yes, fellow Cardinals, a girl who has made herself known not just here at Kennedy but in the world at large as a nationally-ranked figure skater, that sweet and beautiful junior — Lisa Chang!"

Phoebe and Chris looked at each other with complete surprise. They put their hands together and held on hard. "Lisa Chang. . . ." they whispered in amazement.

"Lisa Chang!" Peter roared as he stood outside the control room. Janie Barstow looked around nervously and hinted tentatively that he should lower his voice a little.

"Lisa Chang," he said a little less loudly. "I barely know who she is. What has Lisa Chang ever done for this school?"

Janie looked down at her flat shoes. She didn't like Laurie's maneuverings any better than Peter did, but she did think that Lisa Chang was a nice person. Lisa was in her government class. She always greeted Janie with a smile and never snubbed her like some of the other girls did. In addition, she was a good student and well known for her skating. Sure, she missed a lot of school, but if Lisa was nominated, Janie thought she should be allowed to run.

Peter continued to rant. "I don't think I even remember the last time I saw her in school. Homecoming princess is supposed to be somebody who's done something for Kennedy." He paused and pushed up the sleeves of his army surplus sweater. "Ah, it won't work. Nobody will vote for Lisa, anyway." He sounded as if he were trying to convince himself.

"I don't know," Janie answered reluctantly, "There are always those articles about her in the paper and stuff. I think kids are impressed by her. I mean, she's kind of a glamorous figure." Self-consciously she wrapped her arms around the front of her gray wool jumper, hoping Peter wouldn't mind her disagreeing with him.

Those were not the words Peter wanted to hear, and he brushed away Janie's analysis with a flip of his hand. All he could think was that it was not right, somehow. Everybody in the school knew that Chris deserved to be homecoming princess, and he knew that Laurie held a grudge against her. Obviously Laurie had dug up Lisa as the only girl who had a chance of beating Chris. But if Laurie did manage to win Lisa the crown, it would be for all the wrong reasons. Peter slapped two empty album covers together in disgust and sat down on the floor.

In that same moment, Laurie finished up with her broadcast. She switched off the control switch, and Peter and Janie both saw the "On the Air" light go off above the studio door. Janie noticed that Peter had an expression on his face like a gladiator waiting for the release of a lion.

The studio door swung open, and there Laurie haughtily stood her ground. "Who yelled out here?" she questioned defiantly. "I could actually hear you in the booth. I wouldn't be surprised if the listeners thought there was a mob outside."

"There was a mob outside," Peter shot back,

"a mob consisting of me. Who on student council got the bright idea of nominating Lisa Chang?"

Laurie flicked back her one long earring and looked smugly at Peter. "I did," she said in a deliberately soft voice.

Peter looked disgusted. Janie turned to the shelves that lined the walls and pretended to be filing records.

"Just because Chris Austin has a little competition now. . . ."

"Chris is going to win, because she deserves it," Peter interrupted.

"Is that so?" Laurie shot back.

"And you're just setting Lisa Chang up. The only reason you want Lisa to run is because you want to defeat Chris. Well, it won't work."

Laurie turned and looked at Janie, who was trying her best to disappear into the record shelves.

"What do you think, Janie?"

"Who, me?"

Laurie smiled and nodded. Janie nervously shifted her feet and accidentally dropped an album on the floor. Peter picked it up.

"Go ahead," Laurie insisted, "big, bad Peter can't hurt you for having an opinion."

"Hey, Bennington, cool it. Don't take it out on Janie."

"Well, Janie," Laurie repeated, this time in a voice dipped in honey, "do you think Lisa Chang should be running for homecoming princess or not?"

"Well, I don't know. I mean, she hasn't done stuff for the school like Chris has. . . ."

49

"I repeat, Janie. Do you think Lisa should be able to run?"

"Well, of course. Sure," Janie admitted, "anybody who's nominated can run."

Laurie gave Peter a look of pure triumph. "Well, there you go, Mr. Public Opinion Expert. Let's just let the student body decide."

"They'll decide," vowed Peter, "but you'd better warn Lisa that I'll have some tough questions for her when it comes time to do my interview."

Laurie's eyes blazed. "You just do that, Peter. You may be very surprised."

She then swiftly pushed past Peter and out of the studio.

"I just meant that Lisa had a right to run. I'm sorry," Janie squeaked, trying to ease the situation. But Peter was still fuming. He pulled the studio door shut with a resounding slam and walked quickly down the hall.

Chapter
6

"Excuse me. Oh, I'm really, really sorry."

Laurie Bennington glared at the reedy freshman boy she had edged aside as she swiftly crossed the quad. The skinny boy had just stepped in a huge puddle. It was her fault and *he* was apologizing. They always did. Laurie would have made him apologize again, but she had better things to think about than waterlogged frosh feet. Important things like homecoming and Lisa Chang.

Laurie entered the main building thinking about her latest triumph. Her bid to take the title away from Chris was now a real possibility. Lisa was a good candidate. Chris was popular, good-looking, and respected; but Lisa had been given tremendous publicity because of her skating. If Lisa did a good interview with Peter, and Laurie worked hard to spread the word, there was more than a fair chance that she would win.

It was only fair, Laurie thought, after the way

Chris had spoiled her last party. And the fact that Peter was rooting for Chris only made Laurie's desire for revenge that much stronger. He would pay for rejecting her. They would all pay.

Laurie came to the end of the corridor and turned left. The bell had already rung, and most of the kids were in class, but she had a study hall that period, so she knew she could get away with being late. First she had something to take care of in the student council room. She opened the door.

There were the usual lists and schedules posted on the walls, and on the blackboard was an agenda drawn out for the next meeting. Just as she'd hoped, there was a solitary figure standing at the board. He was checking back and forth between his notes and the blackboard with great concentration.

"Brad!"

"Oh, hi, Laurie," Brad said in a flat voice.

"Getting everything ready?"

Brad nodded. As student body president he had a free period before student council to prepare things.

Laurie looked at him closely. In his red V-neck sweater and neat corduroy pants he looked like the young Princeton student he hoped to become. His straight brown hair was slightly in need of cutting, but the rest was perfect: the button-down shirt, the Bass penny loafers, the intelligent look in his eye. Laurie had always found his clean features and stong build very appealing.

But Brad's handsome features were marked by a sadness, almost a listlessness, that had been with him for several weeks. Laurie knew that had to be what was making Brad so blue. Phoebe. The poor boy was still shell-shocked from the dumping Phoebe had given him over that crazy actor Griffin. Laurie sighed. It would be too easy. It was the perfect time for her to move in.

Laurie adjusted the wide neckline of her knit dress until it slid down to expose the top of one shoulder. With her fingers wedged in her wide leather belt, she walked over to the blackboard to set one hip gently against the wall. She reached out and touched Brad's arm.

"Did you hear my show this afternoon?" she asked in a soft, low voice.

Brad nodded. "A little bit. I was surprised to hear that Lisa's running. She doesn't have much time for school activities, but she's really nice. You know, she's an old friend of Phe . . ." His voice trailed off and he stared at the blackboard. " 'Course, I'm voting for Chris," he added quickly, trying to cover his reference to his old girl friend.

Laurie ignored his comment about Chris. There were more important things on her mind. She tossed back the longer side of her short hair. "I guess this homecoming must be a hard time for you," she said in a creamy voice.

"What do you mean?"

"Phoebe," Laurie said quietly, her eyes rich brown wells of sympathy.

Brad shrugged. "I'm getting over it."

"Good."

53

"Yeah." Brad watched as Laurie pushed one of her sleeves up and a thin gold bracelet slid down her arm.

"I think it's always hard to go to an event that you went to with somebody special. Especially after you break up with that person."

"Yeah," Brad finally admitted. He hit the blackboard lightly with his fist and walked over to sit on top of the nearest desk. He looked down at his hands.

Laurie followed him slowly. "Are you asking anyone to the dance?"

"I don't think so."

Laurie hoisted herself up on the next desk top and let her skirt ride up to the middle of her shapely thighs. "Well, that's silly! The best way to forget is to take somebody else and have a wonderful time. Otherwise, you'll just sit home and mope."

"Maybe you're right," Brad answered absent-mindedly.

"I know I'm right. So you and I will go together. Okay?" Laurie's voice was so bright she might have been a cheerleader.

"Sure," Brad continued in the same, dull tone. Then he looked up quickly as if he wasn't sure what had just been said. "What?" he asked vaguely.

"You and I have a date for homecoming, Brad." Laurie slid off the desk and walked up very close to him.

"We do?"

"We certainly do," she purred. She started to trace his features with her red polished fingertip.

"But Laurie, I. . . ." Brad gulped.

"What's wrong — don't you like me?"

"No, Laur. That's not it."

"Well, then, we'll go to the dance."

"Yeah. Okay. Sure." Brad still looked a little confused, but he was beginning to notice how good-looking Laurie was.

Laurie immediately picked up on his tiny spark of interest. She threw her arms around his neck and pressed against him. "Oh, Brad, I can't wait. We'll have the best time!"

She stepped back and slowly walked to the door, making sure that Brad was following every curvy line. "Till then," she purred. Laurie blew him a kiss and gave him a good-bye look that was meant to make him come running.

After Laurie left, Brad sat on the desk top for a long time and stared into space. "What just happened?" he finally muttered to himself. "What did I just get myself into?"

Chapter
7

"Lisa, aren't you nervous?"

Pam Shumway was whispering across the aisle to Lisa in the middle of Mrs. Perez's algebra II class. Mrs. Perez was explaining a difficult equation, and Lisa was trying her best to concentrate. Usually Lisa was able to ignore Pam's nonstop talking and squirming. But today she couldn't keep her mind on algebra, either.

Pam reached over and tapped Lisa on the elbow. "I think it's really terrific."

"What's that?"

"Your nomination! I decided I'm going to vote for you."

"Thanks." Lisa smiled. "But you haven't even heard my interview yet."

"Isn't it today?"

Lisa nodded but lowered her eyes when she saw Mrs. Perez look her way. A few minutes later she felt Pam slide a note onto the top of her math book.

She unfolded the note and read it.

> Laurie B's been telling everybody to vote for you. Think you will win! Don't worry about interview — won't matter that much. L.B.'s been spreading the word that Peter L. (radio DJ guy) is a creep and does crummy interviews. But he is pretty cute (pant pant).

Pam was looking over at her with a sly smile. Lisa wasn't quite sure what to make of the note and put it away.

Lisa had to admit that lots of kids at school were noticing her now. They were saying hi and congratulating her and wishing her luck. And even though Lisa still felt a little funny about the whole thing, she was excited. She almost felt like a normal person for the first time in her life. It was a very good feeling.

Peter had rushed out of PE to get to the radio station a few minutes early. His hair was still wet and dripping inside the collar of his leather bomber jacket. Peter didn't feel it. He ran across the quad in quick, even strides, preoccupied with his upcoming radio show.

He had been in the middle of a bench press when he'd figured out just how to stop Laurie's attempt to elect Lisa Chang. He thought of all the questions he could ask to make it obvious that Lisa was an inappropriate candidate. Once the idea came to him, the details were easy. Because Lisa *wasn't* a fair candidate. All he had to do was guide the interview so that the facts were made clear.

Peter raced into the control room, whipped off his jacket, and sat in front of the board. Pulling his notebook out of his gray knapsack, he began to write furiously. He wrote out his questions in a big, clear hand. He wanted to be able to read his notes easily while he was on the air.

Just as he was about to finish, he heard the relentless click of high-heeled boots. He knew who it was even before she walked in.

"You'd better give Lisa a fair interview!" Laurie stood glaring in the doorway, a cashmere sweater slung carelessly over one shoulder.

Peter tried to ignore her and continued writing.

"You'd better not try anything slimy," Laurie went on.

"Cool it, Laur," Peter replied. Laurie obviously didn't like being ignored.

"You know what I mean," Laurie threatened.

Peter lifted his head and ran his hand through his damp, wavy hair. "I'll be just as fair and sweet as you are on the radio, Laur," Peter came back sarcastically. He took a deep breath and went back to his notebook.

Laurie shifted her terrific body and pulled up the top of one of her suede boots. "Yesterday you were so nice to that boring Caroline Macy, I thought you were going to ask her to marry you."

Laurie was really pushing it today, Peter thought. "It happens to be my job to make sure

58

the interviews are good. Besides, Caroline is a very nice person and she's done a heck of a lot for this school. Geez, Laur, if you're so gung ho about making sure that Chris doesn't win the crown, I'd think you'd thank me for making Caroline's interview so interesting."

"Macy's a loser," Laurie pronounced. "Six months from now she'll gain back all that weight and be as fat as a cow again."

Peter winced. Obviously Laurie wanted not only to defeat Chris, but also to heap scorn on any other girl who didn't meet her ridiculous criteria. Peter couldn't help wondering how Lisa Chang had gotten in so well with Laurie. That thought made him really want to nail Lisa over the air.

"Bennington, you wouldn't even know the meaning of *decent* if you looked it up in the dictionary."

Just at that moment Janie hesitantly scooted past Laurie and put three albums in the rack over the control panel. She wore a baggy wool skirt and matching cardigan sweater. Laurie looked at Janie as though the tall, shy girl had just brought in a sack of decaying fruit.

"Hi," Janie whispered softly and turned back to the overhead rack. She checked the records already there, pulling a few out and setting them on top of the control board.

Laurie ignored her. "Peter, if you think Caroline Macy is so wonderful, why don't you take her to homecoming? I'm sure she doesn't have a date."

Janie gave Laurie a quick, concerned glance

59

but was relieved to hear Peter exhale disgustedly. Janie couldn't imagine Peter liking Caroline Macy.

"C'mon, Peter, I know a clod like you doesn't have a date," Laurie added nastily.

"That's right. Me and Janie are just going to have to slave away at the music. Gee, maybe they'll let the two of us be the chaperones. Right, partner?" Peter gave Janie a wink.

Janie realized that Laurie was staring at her. She grabbed her records, pushed past Laurie, and fled out into the hall.

"Hey, what about you, Bennington?" Peter remembered what Janie had told him about Laurie's expensive outfit. "I hear you can't find anybody who can stand an evening with you, either."

Laurie grinned. "Is that so?"

"Is it?"

"Well, it just so happens that I am going to homecoming with the student body president." She let her statement sit there like a time bomb and waited for Peter to react. A stunned silence filled the tiny studio.

"Brad asked you to the dance. . . ." Peter finally said in an amazed voice.

"Mm-hmm," Laurie purred. "He sure did."

By the time Lisa walked in, Peter and Laurie were no longer speaking. Lisa sensed the tension, but she was overwhelmed by her own nervousness and excitement. Then, when Peter turned in his chair to look at her, she felt something else. It started at the base of her spine and ran up the back of her neck. It was something like a tingle,

60

but not quite. As long as he looked at her, the tingly feeling kept going. Pam Shumway had been right about one thing: Peter was very attractive.

Peter was still staring at her. His eyes were green, and his mouth was curling slightly in an involuntary smile. There was a sense of time being suspended for a moment, until Laurie's sharp voice pierced the air and everything speeded up again.

"Lisa, this is Peter Lacey. He is going to interview you, and I'm sure he will control his usual creepish tendencies and be very nice." Laurie's tone was harsh. Lisa had never seen this side of Laurie before.

"Laurie, thank you; you can leave now." Peter practically pushed Laurie out into the hall.

"Okay, but I'm going out to the quad where I can listen, and you'd better not try anything sleazy," Laurie warned in a fierce whisper.

Lisa wasn't sure what to make of the obvious dislike between Laurie and Peter and tried not to let it bother her. Peter stepped back into the control room. He pulled another chair over for Lisa, and she sat down.

Lisa watched Peter push some buttons. Every few seconds he would turn and look back at her. He seemed to be about to say something, but he never did. Finally he grabbed a sheet of notebook paper that was covered with writing and placed it in front of him.

"Are you ready?" he asked edgily.

"I guess," Lisa managed. She didn't know what to expect but hoped to give a good interview. With fascination she watched as Peter spun around in his chair, flicked a switch, and checked a turntable. He grabbed two pairs of lightweight earphones and hung one around his neck.

"You need to wear these."

Peter leaned toward her. Lisa started to take the earphones from him, but instead he moved closer and put them over her ears himself. His face was very close to hers. Again he stopped and stared at her with the strangest, searching look. Lisa wasn't sure what it meant, but it made her feel flushed and breathless.

Peter backed away, cleared his throat, then spun around again to take out a record. Finally he flipped on the microphone with one graceful motion.

"Hello, Cardinals. This is Peter Lacey, your man at WKND here with another day of homecoming specials. This week, I've been interviewing the candidates for junior princess. Today we have Lisa Chang. Hello, Lisa," Peter looked at Lisa to let her know it was her turn to talk.

"Hi."

There was a short silence. Lisa noticed that Peter was also a little nervous. Suddenly he looked away from her and shook his head, as if annoyed at himself about something. He grabbed at his piece of paper, which Lisa saw had a list of questions. She took a deep breath and prepared herself.

Peter began in a controlled, professional tone. "Lisa, as you know, a homecoming princess is supposed to be someone who is not only popular but has also made a real contribution to Kennedy

High. Would you tell us exactly which school activities you've been involved in?" His glance wouldn't meet hers.

Lisa wasn't sure what to answer for a moment. She had never been in any school activities, and surely Peter knew that. Why was he asking her?

"I'm mainly involved with my classes . . . if that's what you mean."

"I see." Peter nodded, always looking down at his sheet of questions.

"What do you think of the football team this season? Do you think they have a chance at the championship?"

Lisa grew tense. Was Peter intentionally asking her things he knew she wouldn't be able to answer? She gave Peter a pleading look, but he was still staring down at his notes. "I guess I don't know about that. I spend most of my time in training. I ice skate —"

Peter cut her off and read from his questions again. "Would you tell us what school offices you have held?"

Lisa was beginning to feel like a fool. She didn't answer.

Peter prompted her. "For instance, Chris Austin is head of the honor society; Caroline Macy is president of the service —"

"I didn't know Chris was running," Lisa blurted out. With so much extra practice the last few days, she hadn't even found out who else was in the contest. She had never thought that she'd be running against one of her old friends. She was beginning to feel as if she hadn't given any real thought to what she was getting involved with. She tried to regain her composure, but Peter threw another question at her.

"How about the fund-raiser last year to build the new handball courts. Did you work on that?"

"No."

"I see. Do you belong to any school clubs?"

"No."

"Kennedy athletics?"

"Not really. I'm not on a team."

"Obviously you have not been very involved in school. How about the community? Have you done volunteer work at the hospital?"

"No, I. . . ."

"Local politics?"

Lisa didn't answer.

"The can drive at Christmas?"

"I brought cans and clothes down to the shelter in Carlton."

"Did you stay and volunteer your time at the shelter or just drop stuff off?"

Lisa felt like she was being attacked. "I just dropped stuff off. Look, I guess if girls like Chris or Caroline are running, I don't really deserve it. I'm not involved in much stuff at school or in the community. But it's not that I don't want to be or I don't care. Since I was six years old I've spent more than half of every day in an ice rink or at dance classes training to be a figure skater. If I hadn't, I wouldn't be any good. So there hasn't been much time for anything else. I wish there had been. Believe me, I've missed not being a part of things here at school and in town."

Suddenly Peter's posture changed. He sat up

straighter and pushed his list of questions off the edge of the board. The paper floated silently to the floor. Lisa wasn't sure what had happened to change Peter's attitude, but he now looked a little embarrassed, as if, hearing her words, he'd finally realized how unfairly he had been treating her. When he spoke again, his voice was very different. It was much more sympathetic.

"Do you miss having a normal life?"

"Sometimes. But not when I really think about it. Most of the time I love skating, and I think I'm really lucky to be able to do it. I hope I can still be a well-rounded person, and I worry sometimes that I'll become too lopsided. You know, just obsessed with skating. I do miss my old friends."

Peter finally looked at her and gave a nervous smile. He had definitely dropped his hostile questioning, but Lisa couldn't figure out why.

"Lisa, what do you think being a skater has taught you?" Peter's eyes were now focused intently on hers.

"I think skating has taught me that you have to work really hard to achieve something. And that there are always going to be things that you have to give up, even though you may not want to."

Through the little window to the control room, Janie Barstow signaled that time was running out. Peter looked bothered, but Lisa was grateful that the interview was almost over. It hadn't gone at all the way she'd hoped, even though Peter had let up toward the end.

"One last question, Lisa. This is one every

girl has to answer. Why do you think you should be chosen princess?"

"I'm not sure I should be chosen." Lisa felt a strong need to explain herself. "But I was nominated, and it's kind of nice to be involved. I don't expect to win, but it's fun and I'm flattered that someone thought of me."

"Okay, there you have it, Cardinals. One of your nominees for homecoming princess, Lisa Chang. Now, getting back to some music, I have a platter cued up here on turntable one. A little something by the Rockets."

Lisa stood up before Peter turned back around. She was very angry and confused. Peter had asked her intentionally difficult questions and then let her flounder. Then he'd suddenly changed toward the end of the interview, after he had definitely set out to make her come off badly. Was it to make himself seem like a good guy? Was this the way kids treated each other? Maybe she had been lucky to have missed out on a high-school social life.

When Peter turned to face her again, Lisa began to feel even more mixed-up and hurt. She just wanted to get away from the radio station, away from school, back to the rink. Even going back and skating her circles was better than being treated like this. Pam Shumway was right. Peter was a creep who did lousy interviews. With an abrupt gesture, Lisa grabbed her book bag. As she pushed open the control room door, she felt Peter's hand on her arm.

"Lisa. . . ."

"Good-bye," she said tightly. "I'm late for practice."

Lisa was not the only one who was upset and confused. As Peter watched her angrily walk away, his head began to pound. He waited for Lisa to turn back around, to stop and reconsider. No such luck. She was definitely gone.

"You big jerk, Lacey," Peter muttered to himself.

Two minutes later, Laurie Bennington came flying down the hall. She swooped into the studio and leaned over Peter who was now sitting pensively at the control board.

"Where's Lisa?" she demanded.

"She left already."

"Well, smart face, your devious plan backfired!" Laurie smiled victoriously.

"What?"

"Your sleazoid plan to make Lisa sound like a fool. Asking her about volunteering at that gross shelter. Well, guess what everybody thought?"

Peter looked up. He didn't know. But he was sure that Laurie had carefully guided everyone's opinion.

"Everybody listening in the quad thought that you were nasty and unfair to Lisa. They also thought that she was incredibly sweet and humble, and they all loved her. You may just have won the election for her with that lousy interview."

"Huh?"

Laurie didn't miss a beat. "Because now everybody feels sorry for her. You acted like such a creep. Lisa's chances of beating Chris just keep getting better and better!"

With that, Laurie tossed her one long earring and stomped out of the studio. She slammed the door behind her with an arrogant swing of her shoulders and sauntered down the hall.

But Peter barely heard her. Like a robot, he brought up the next record and slid back down into his chair. What had he just done? He had allowed his anger at Laurie to make him mess up something he really loved — the radio station. His job was to make the girls sound as good as possible, not to expose their faults.

And Lisa . . . When Peter thought of her, he got a knot in the middle of his chest. She had fended off his dumb questions with honesty and grace. Now she probably thought he was an insensitive jerk. And he had been, during most of the interview. As soon as he'd realized what he was doing, he'd changed his tactics, but by then it was too late. He'd blown it. That thought bothered Peter most of all. That and the fact that Lisa Chang probably never wanted to speak to him again.

Chapter
8

Whack!

Lisa slammed shut the door of her locker and sat on the long, narrow bench. The ice rink dressing room was quiet, and the angry noise echoed off the gray concrete walls.

She pulled her white skates on and began to lace them with swift, deliberate strokes. She was beginning to regret having gotten involved in the whole homecoming princess business. What made her think she could just step in and take part in such an important school activity? Peter Lacey certainly felt that her candidacy was a joke. Her interview had proven that. True, Peter had softened toward the end of their talk, but not before he'd made his point. It was stupid for Lisa to pretend that she was just like other kids.

She put her pink sweater back on over a white cotton turtleneck and pulled hard at her beige tights to readjust them.

"Darn!" She'd poked her finger right through the thin nylon. She slunk down on the bench and watched several tiny runs race down her thigh. With disgust she began to unlace her skates.

What was the matter with her? Coach Bielman was coming to watch her Monday afternoon. This was one of the last afternoons she had to practice before he came, and she was so frazzled that she couldn't even get dressed!

She peeled off the torn tights and unwrapped a brand-new pair. Her legs bare, she stared at the Ace bandage that was wrapped tightly around her left ankle. Another thing to worry about. Gingerly, she poked the area behind her ankle where the injury had occurred. No pain. At least not now. But she knew that it could very well flare up again when she least expected it.

She pulled her new white tights over her muscular legs and tried to relax. She had to get hold of herself and not let things at school ruin her concentration. That was what would make or break her chances with Bielman. It was that simple.

"Peter!" Lisa muttered.

She sat still for a second. She was disturbed to realize that Peter Lacey was still on her mind. She could see him clearly — his dark, wavy hair, curious green eyes, strong arms. When he had leaned close to help her put on her earphones, she had felt her heart speed up and her face get warm. But then he had purposely tried to make her sound like someone who didn't belong, someone who was an outsider. It was like skating her circles again. She went around and around, but

70

she never really got anywhere and never broke free.

Lisa replaced her skates, slipped on a pair of white gloves, and walked out into the rink. The tinny music coming over the sound system was muted and blended easily with the swooshing and gliding of skate blades. There were no more than a dozen skaters on the ice, including a gifted ten-year-old girl and three college hockey players. In one corner, Rick was giving a lesson to a middle-aged woman. He patiently guided the woman around the ice, almost like a father encouraging his child's first steps. Lisa faced the ice and did her warm-up exercises.

"Lisa, you are late!" lectured Mr. Helde as he walked toward her. He wore black pants and an old Norwegian ski sweater.

"Didn't my mom tell you I had to do something special at school today?"

"Oh, ya." Mr. Helde tugged on his mustache. "I forgot." He patted her on the shoulder. "You have your music on from two-thirty to three-thirty."

"Okay." Lisa nodded. That meant that Mr. Helde would play the music that she would be using for her freestyle routine for Bielman. By the rules of the rink, the other skaters would give her right-of-way while she rehearsed her short and long routines.

"Thanks."

"Ya." Mr. Helde smiled and padded back to his office near the front entrance.

Lisa watched him retreat and wondered what she would do if Bielman didn't take her. This was an important step. If Bielman said no, Lisa's skating probably wouldn't go much further. Then what would she do? Go back to school full-time? Be a normal Rose Hill teenager? Lisa didn't think that idea was too promising. Not after today. Peter had made her see that.

She slipped off her skate guards and stroked her way around the ice. She felt so anxious and tense, and yet she knew that if she wanted to excel Monday, the last thing she should be doing was worrying. That was the one thing that would surely cause her to fail. It was the old *Catch 22*: the more she worried the worse she would do. But when she consciously tried not to worry, she got worried about worrying. Lisa continued to skate in strong, even glides and wished she could forget about everything.

Chris was waiting for Phoebe after school to get a ride home. The day was brisk and cool. Chris's silky blonde hair was blowing gently across her face. She looked across the congested parking lot and could see just the edge of the athletic field where Ted was at football practice. It was too far off to make him out, but she smiled as she thought about him speeding and weaving in his muddy white pants and bright red Cardinal jersey. She was so happy that she and Ted were back together again.

Standing up to get a better view, Chris thought she recognized a distant figure wandering slowly along the far side of the parking lot. The girl was walking with her head down, as if she didn't want anybody to notice her.

"Brenda!" Chris yelled. Her stepsister stopped at the sound of her name and looked around. Chris waved vigorously until Brenda spotted her. Brenda stood still and waited for Chris to run over to her.

"Hi," Chris panted. "Phoebe's driving me home. Want a lift?"

Brenda kept her head down and let her layered dark hair fall around her face. She was wearing a pair of dark glasses that Chris hadn't seen on her in some time. After snapping up the front of her jeans jacket, Brenda stuck her hands in the pockets of her short denim skirt. Chris wondered if Brenda had been crying.

"Bren, what's the matter?" Chris asked with great concern.

"Nothing," Brenda said defensively with a catch in her voice.

"I don't believe that. Come on. Come home with me and Phoebe and we'll talk about it." Brenda didn't move. "Please," Chris urged.

Brenda shrugged sullenly and gave a half nod. Silently she followed her stepsister back across the parking lot. When they got to the flagpole, the sisters sat next to each other on the concrete retaining wall.

"You'd better be careful," Brenda said finally in her low, smoky voice. "Don't let anybody see you with me. That is, not if you want to win for homecoming princess." Brenda's tone was resentful and sarcastic.

"What do you mean?" Chris asked with confusion.

Brenda looked around to see if anyone could

overhear. "Oh, forget it," she said disgustedly. She started to get up and walk away.

"No, I won't forget it," Chris insisted. "Tell me what happened." She was holding on to Brenda's slender arm.

The crowds were starting to thin out as scores of cars zoomed out of the lot. Even the buses were beginning to pull out.

"You wouldn't understand."

"Try me." Chris stood very straight and pulled down her argyle sweater vest.

"All right," Brenda sighed finally. She slid her glasses to the top of her head. "You know Mr. Sholeson?"

Chris nodded. Sholeson was Brenda's history teacher, and he was known for being one of the toughest teachers at their top high school.

"Well, we got our last test back today and, um, I got a B plus." Brenda looked away as if she were embarrassed.

"Brenda, that's great! Especially coming from Sholeson. Congratulations."

"Yeah," Brenda answered disgustedly. "Anyway, Sholeson sort of told whole class — you know, when he passed the papers back — that he was pleased that I did so well."

"Yes."

"Then I went to the bathroom after class, and I overheard a bunch of girls talking. . . ." Brenda's voice started to catch again.

"And," Chris prompted.

"Well, I don't know who they all were, but I recognized Laurie Bennington, for sure."

"Oh, no."

"So some girl was talking about how hard the test was and how I got such a good grade. And Laurie told them all that I must have cheated to do that well. . . ."

Brenda was fighting tears, and Chris put a hand on her wrist.

"Because everyone knew that I was dishonest!"

Chris was feeling sick. Why couldn't Laurie leave her sister alone? It was hard enough for Brenda to work her way into the social life at Kennedy. Especially since kids knew about how she'd run away. But people were starting to forget about that by now, and every day Brenda was doing better. Now Laurie was trying to drag her down again.

"Did you let her know you were there? Did you say anything?"

"I was going to, but then she started talking about you."

"Oh?"

"She told them about your getting drunk at her last party and how now you were hanging out with me. She said that means that you're turning into a sleaze, too, and that if you're elected homecoming princess it'll be a disgrace." Brenda took a deep breath and slipped her dark glasses back down over her eyes.

Chris was steaming! She didn't care what Laurie said about her. As far as the incident of her getting drunk, it was so unlike Chris that most kids wouldn't believe it anyway. And the kids who did believe it wouldn't really care. Besides, it was true. But lying about Brenda . . . who was trying so hard to put her life back together

. . . well, that was hitting below the belt. Chris had to do something to stop it. She owed it to her sister.

"Brenda, I'm really sorry."

"It's not your fault," Brenda said hoarsely.

The two sisters heard a loud hello behind them and saw Phoebe walking out of the main building. In her funky man's shirt and bow tie she looked puckish and cheerful. But she immediately noticed the gloom on Chris and Brenda's faces.

"What's the matter?"

Chris could sense that Brenda didn't feel comfortable talking in front of Phoebe. "I'll tell you later," she whispered.

"Brenda, you want a ride home?" Phoebe asked sweetly.

Brenda hesitated. "No, thanks. I think I'm going to go to Georgetown. I need to talk to somebody there."

Chris knew that Brenda was going to talk to her friends at the halfway house. At one time Chris and her parents had looked down on Brenda's continued attachment to Garfield House — the halfway house for runaways that Brenda had gone to after she'd left home the year before. But Chris had come to realize that the association wasn't necessarily so bad, and she had convinced her parents to be more tolerant.

"I'll drive you down there. I don't mind," Phoebe offered.

"Thanks, but I'd rather take the bus. I kind of feel like being alone."

"If you're sure," Phoebe questioned.

"Yeah. Chris, tell Mom where I went and that I'll be home by dinnertime."

"Okay," Chris agreed.

The two friends watched as Brenda slowly wandered off, then they turned toward Phoebe's mom's station wagon.

"Sorry I took so long. Woody got a postcard from Griffin, and I wanted to see it. Then we started talking, and you know how Woody can yak." Phoebe could tell that Chris wasn't listening to her. "What's going on, Chris?"

"Laurie Bennington," Chris spat out angrily. "I have to find a way to stop her!"

Chapter
9

Peter pulled his Vokswagen into the parking lot of the Capitol Ice Rink. He flipped off the cassette deck and grabbed Lisa's math book from the frayed seat next to him. She had forgotten it at the radio station that afternoon.

No one was at the rink's front desk, so Peter just wandered in. He stared up at the corrugated metal ceiling and took in the colorful flags that hung from each corner. Again, no one seemed to notice him, so he decided to sit and watch.

He climbed up to one of the top benches, shivered, and pulled his dark brown bomber jacket closed. Boy, it was cold. Immediately he spotted Lisa. It was impossible not to. The whole rink seemed to revolve around her. An echoey Gershwin recording was blasting over the loudspeakers and Lisa was in the midst of rehearsing an elaborate routine.

Peter was astonished. She could go so fast with

such control, especially in such a tiny area. It reminded him of a model he'd once seen of an electron bouncing around in space. Lisa was just like that — swift, always moving around and around, creating lots of energy.

Her dark, beautiful hair flew back and forth as if it were being tossed in the wind. Her delicate, exotic features were set and cool. It was like pictures Peter had seen of models in fashion magazines, but in those pictures you knew that the model was standing in front of a big fan and the photographer was taking dozens of photos until he found the one that was just right. There was nothing posed or still about what Lisa was doing. When she did come to a stop, the flying ice chips and the scraping of her skates reminded him just how fast she had been moving.

After the music finished, Lisa skated over to the side barrier with her hands on her hips. She barely looked up into the stands; it was as if she were totally and completely alone. Peter understood that feeling. He knew it from the radio station. He could shut out the world and simply talk to his listeners. But Peter always took great pleasure in those moments of privacy and concentration. In contrast, Lisa's face was tight with tension, and she looked as though she was forcing herself to keep on going.

She skated back to the far corner, and with intense purpose worked on one difficult move. Over and over she jumped and spun — so quickly that Peter gasped, fearing that she might fall. She didn't, but each time she came out of the jump she shook her head as if angry with herself.

Finally, she did the jump perfectly, and it was breathtaking.

Peter didn't know how, but whatever the flaw was, Lisa had conquered it. She showed a brief moment of relief but quickly began to circle the rink again with her hands on her hips. She looked tired. There was no joy, no elation, no sign that she was really pleased with what she'd done. *That's wrong*, Peter thought to himself. *Wrong!* He walked down to the rink edge and leaned against the railing.

Gliding around the rink, hands on hips, Lisa looked up and blinked her eyes.

"Peter."

She was very surprised. There he was in his brown leather jacket, T-shirt, and jeans, his dark wavy hair framing his handsome face. What was he doing there? Lisa felt a surge of humiliation as she looked at him leaning uncomfortably against the side of the rink. Had he come to let her know just how bad an idea it was for her to be involved in the homecoming contest?

In spite of the way she felt, Lisa found herself skating over to him. She ran her hand along the railing and gave Peter a suspicious glare. He actually looked a little nervous as she came close and couldn't quite meet her eye.

"Hi," he said tensely.

"Hi," Lisa answered drily.

Neither of them said anything for a minute or so. Uncomfortable, Lisa started to push off and rejoin the flow of skaters around the rink.

"Wait," Peter urged.

Lisa felt his hand rest gently on her arm. She

80

stopped curtly and faced him again.

"You forgot your math book at the station," Peter said softly. He held up the textbook.

Lisa looked him fully in the eye for the first time. His cheeks were a little red from the cold air. "Thanks."

"Sure. I thought you might need it tonight. Big test tomorrow or something."

Lisa didn't respond. She took the book and leaned over the railing to place it on the bench. Peter tried to help her, but it was an awkward gesture.

"Lisa, can you take a break for a few minutes? I want to talk to you."

Lisa looked around. Shelley Baird's music was playing now. Lisa's ice time was nearly finished. The question remained — what did Peter want?

"I don't know. I don't usually interrupt my practice. . . ."

"Please," Peter pleaded, "no microphones this time." Lisa glanced over to where her coach often sat watching her, but he had returned to his office.

"All right. Just a few minutes." Lisa motioned ahead. There was something in Peter's posture that made her want to hear what he had to say. She led the way to the snack shop and sat down at the corner table.

"You want something to drink?" Peter asked.

"No, thanks."

Rubbing his hands together, Peter sat down across from her. "Cold in here," he said.

"Yes."

Peter moved his head as if he were wearing a collar that was too tight. Finally he looked at

Lisa and took a deep breath. "The real reason I came to see you . . . I mean I wanted to give you back your book and everything . . . but mostly I wanted to say something about our interview this afternoon."

"What?"

"Well, mostly that I did a crummy job and I tried to make you sound bad and it was totally unfair. It was my fault, and I'm really sorry." He spoke quickly, as if he wanted to get it over with.

Lisa could hardly believe her ears. Peter seemed to sense her skepticism and nervously fingered a sugar bowl. "I really am sorry," he repeated.

Lisa was amazed to hear him apologize. He truly seemed as upset about the whole thing as she was.

Peter shifted in his chair. "I guess the people who heard you figured that I was just being a jerk and you handled me real well. So don't worry about it." He nodded his head for emphasis.

"Then you *did* do it on purpose. You really wanted me to sound bad."

"Yeah. I wrote out all the questions I knew you couldn't answer."

"But why?"

Peter shook his head disgustedly. "It has nothing to do with you. It was so stupid. I was mad at Bennington, so I took it out on you. I guess I thought you and Laurie were really tight or something." Peter gave her a look as if he wanted confirmation. Was Lisa a good friend of Laurie's or not?

"I barely know Laurie. She asked me if I'd run and I said I would."

"Yeah. I figured that . . . later . . . after the interview. Actually, toward the end. I still don't believe I did it. Man, I am really sorry."

The look on Peter's face was one of dead earnest. Lisa couldn't believe he cared so much about a contest for homecoming princess.

"Lisa, as soon as you came into the studio I knew you weren't like Laurie, but I had all those questions planned and I got nervous or something —" Peter looked away and cleared his throat "— and I didn't think very well."

Lisa felt her anger melting away. "I guess it's pretty easy to get nervous on the air. I know I was."

"Yeah, well, I haven't been nervous on the air for the entire last year." Peter looked at her and gave a tiny smile.

Lisa couldn't help smiling, too. She saw the beginning of a playful glint in Peter's eye, and she felt herself responding to it. "I guess it's not really that big a deal."

Peter took a deep breath. "Lisa, I hurt your feelings, and that's a major deal." He paused to look at her. "I really care about the radio station. I love it. And my job is to make all the interviews as good as they can be. I don't like it when I get hung up on the wrong kind of stuff. Then, my show is just a waste, a total waste."

"What do you mean, the wrong stuff?"

"I wasn't doing my job, thinking about the right things. If I'd really been doing my job in that interview I wouldn't have worried about Laurie because I would have been concentrating entirely on getting to know you. If I'd done that, there would have been no way the interview could have been anything less than great." Peter's voice was now warm and quick. He looked down at his hands and smiled.

Lisa laughed softly. When Peter finally looked up, he met her eyes. They both smiled and looked away. There was a long pause.

Lisa looked up at Peter again, and this time his eyes stayed on hers for a long time. It was as though they were taking each other in. Peter's green eyes were full of warmth, and interest, and a funny kind of wisdom. Lisa suddenly sensed that Peter was someone who would understand the way that she saw the world. He seemed to feel the same way about his radio station as she did about her skating, and that was a bond that made her want to open up and share herself.

"I wonder if I'm making the same mistake with my skating.

"What do you mean?"

"Like you said. Concentrating on the wrong things. Or not concentrating on the right things. I understand how you feel about the radio station. That's how I used to feel about this ice rink. But lately I don't love it as much as I did." Lisa halted. She had never really talked about this with anyone before.

"Why?"

"I guess because I'm thinking about how I have to win — you know, in competitions. And then when I think about winning, I start to think about losing and all the things that could happen to make me lose, and pretty soon I'm skating badly. . . ."

"And you do lose."

"Right. Or like next Monday, this very important coach is coming to watch me. If he thinks I'm good enough, he'll ask me to go to his training center in Colorado and work with him, and that would be a huge step for me. But all I do is worry that he's not going to like me, or that my mom will be disappointed, or that he won't take me and then what will I do?"

"Why do you want to skate, anyway?"

Lisa was bewildered by the question. It had been so long since she had thought about it. It took a moment to answer. "When I was little, I just skated because I thought it was the best thing to do in the entire world." Lisa's face broke into an involuntary smile as she thought back. "My parents had to drag me away from the rink. I loved it. I guess now with competing and worrying about scores, and Coach Bielman, sometimes the pressure just gets to me."

Peter was listening intently. All his energy was focused on her.

"Lisa, all I know is that if you don't love something you shouldn't do it — at least something like skating or being a DJ. The love of doing it is the main reason *to* do it. The working at it and figuring it out and sometimes getting it right — that's what's fun. And if you just think about those things . . . well, then you have to do a good job. Does that make sense?"

Lisa opened her eyes wide. "I'm not sure."

"Like me. If I go on the radio to get back at Laurie Bennington, I do a lousy job. Right? Okay, if I just go on because I love to do it, and

I care about it and it's fun, then I do a great job. See? So maybe instead of thinking about winning, or worrying about this big-time coach, you should just skate because you love it. Like when you were a kid. What's the worst that can happen? You lose. This guy doesn't take you. Well, if all you do is worry, it's definite you're gonna lose. Right?"

"Right!" Suddenly it made so much sense. Peter was absolutely right. Lisa laughed and peeled off her knit gloves. There was a short pause. "I'll try and think that way when I practice this weekend."

"Great."

Again they were silent. Then they both started to laugh at the same time.

"Hey, Lisa!" a voice suddenly broke in.

Lisa looked up to see Rick and Shelley standing in front of her table. They were looking at Peter with a curious expression. Lisa wondered what time it was and how long she and Peter had been talking.

"Lis, your mom's waiting outside," Rick said. He took Shelley's skate bag from her.

"Thanks. Tell her I'll be out in a minute."

"Sure thing." Rick gave Peter another good look before he and Shelley left.

"Well, I guess I have to go. . . ." Lisa started to stand up, when she felt Peter's hand on hers.

"So you forgive me?" he asked, his green eyes not leaving her face for a second.

"I forgive you."

"I'm really glad." Peter let go of her hand and

86

walked to the snack shop exit. He leaned against the door. "You have to practice all weekend?"

"Yeah."

"Because that coach is coming Monday?"

"Uh-huh."

"Have a good practice."

"Okay."

"See you."

" 'Bye."

"G'bye."

Peter still stood in the doorway. It took the longest time for him to turn and open the door. Finally he did, but it was too bad, Lisa thought. She wouldn't have minded if Peter had stood there forever.

Chapter 10

"I'll kill her if she does one more thing to hurt Brenda," Chris ranted as she slapped the tennis ball. It sailed across the net with fierce determination.

Phoebe swung awkwardly and watched the ball bounce by her. She pushed up the sleeves of her sweat shirt and trotted toward the fence to retrieve it. Wiping her forehead and pushing back her red hair, Phoebe sighed.

"Let's walk home and talk about it. That's the fifth ball in a row I've missed. . . ."

"Okay," Chris conceded. She picked up her can of tennis balls and pulled on a heavy cable-knit sweater. It was getting cold, anyway, and two boys were waiting impatiently for the court. Besides, it would be easier to talk without a net between them, and Chris needed to talk.

Phoebe slipped on her blue satin warm-up jacket. It had her name embroidered on the front and "Kennedy Follies" on the back. Woody had arranged for everyone who'd been in the school talent show to order one.

"Am I playing any better at all?" Phoebe asked doubtfully. It was the third tennis lesson Chris had given her after school at Rose Hill Park. Phoebe was a rotten tennis player, but at least it helped keep her mind off Griffin and Brad.

"Mmm," Chris answered absentmindedly. She looked toward the baseball diamond and tapped her racket against her thigh.

Phoebe started to laugh. "Sure. Watch out, Chris Evert Lloyd, right?"

"Huh?" Chris responded. "What?"

"Forget it. Nothing. Let's go," Phoebe said easily. Both girls walked quickly off the court and onto the grass. Phoebe kicked her way through the piles of fallen leaves and headed for the street.

"So what did Laurie do now?" Phoebe asked. She swung her racket at an imaginary ball.

Chris shook her head. "It was bad enough when she was reminding kids that Brenda ran away from home last year. But today Ted told me that some kids were saying that they heard that Brenda does drugs. I'm sure Laurie started that one. This just keeps getting worse. It's not fair."

Phoebe walked quickly to keep up with Chris's angry stride. "Well, what can you do about it?"

"I don't know. The only reason Laurie's doing it is to get back at me, to try to keep me from winning homecoming princess. Brenda is an innocent bystander. Maybe I should just drop out of the race. I should just let Lisa or somebody else have it."

"But that's what Laurie wants, Chris. That's just giving in to her."

"You're right, but what am I supposed to do? Tomorrow I have to go on the radio for that interview with Peter. Am I just supposed to tell everybody what a great candidate I am and pretend that nothing weird is going on?"

The best friends continued to walk. They were both deep in thought, trying to figure out how to solve the problem. Three long blocks later they wandered into the circular driveway in front of Phoebe's house. Phoebe waved to her mother who was standing at the kitchen window and then leaned against the stocky oak tree that dominated her front yard. Chris stood in front of her and balanced the can of balls on her racket.

Suddenly Chris put the can and racket down. "I have an idea."

"You do?"

"I've got to face up to Laurie."

"What do you mean?" Phoebe leaned forward.

"Over the radio. If Laurie can use her time on the radio to say nasty things about people, then I can use my princess interview tomorrow to set things straight."

"Chris, that's a great idea!"

Chris's face was set in concentration. "I have to figure out how to do this so Brenda won't get mad at me, either. You know how sensitive she is."

"Well, Austin," teased Phoebe, "figure it out.

You're not head of the honor society for nothing!"

Chris smiled. "I wish Ted could help me plan what to say, but he has some big essay due tomorrow."

"I'm sure you'll manage fine," Phoebe encouraged.

At that moment Phoebe's front door opened and Mrs. Hall appeared. Her short, curly hair was a toned-down version of Phoebe's, and she had a round, kindly face.

"Hello, Chris. Phoebe, sweetheart, telephone." Mrs. Hall dried her hands on her print apron and disappeared back into the house.

Phoebe looked at Chris to make sure that Chris wasn't still upset.

"Go on in, Pheeb. It's okay. I have it under control. Talk to you tonight or else see you tomorrow at school."

Phoebe handed Chris back her borrowed racket and headed toward the house. "Okay. 'Bye." She waved. Chris waved back and began to jog away.

Phoebe walked into the warm house and stopped to take off her jacket. It was probably Woody or Sasha on the phone. Her mother was at the counter in front of the window stirring a large bowlful of cookie dough. Phoebe leaned over and casually picked up the receiver.

"Hello," she said spiritedly as she pulled the phone across to the middle of the kitchen. She stuck her finger in the bowl of cookie dough. Her mother slapped her hand, but not until Phoebe had stuck a fingerful in her mouth. Then she heard the male voice come over the line.

"Phoebe?"

Phoebe's heart stopped, and the sugary dough caught in her throat. The voice was a little fuzzy and far away, but there was no mistaking Griffin Neill.

"Griffin?" Phoebe felt her cheeks redden and saw her mother raise her eyes. "Mom, can I use the phone in your room?"

Mrs. Hall nodded.

"Griffin, hold on. I'm just going to switch phones, okay?" Phoebe set the cradle on the desk and tore down the hallway. When she reached her parents' bedroom she picked up the phone and threw herself back on the king-size bed.

"Okay, Mom. Thanks," Phoebe said and waited for the click as her mom hung up the other phone.

"Phoebe! Hi! It's so great to hear your voice!"

"It's so great to hear yours!" Phoebe smiled. "I miss you."

"I miss you, too," Griffin echoed. His voice was strong and filled with excitement.

Just hearing Griffin brought it all back to Phoebe. She could see his gray-blue eyes, shaggy brown hair, that look on his face that alternated between curiosity and wonder. She could feel the way he used to hold her, with such urgency and care. She missed him so much.

"I didn't think it would be you. You said you weren't going to call until next week." Phoebe wasn't that surprised, though. She and Griffin usually weren't able to wait for the dates they made to call each other. But Griffin had never called in the late afternoon before. He always waited until after eleven at night when it was less expensive.

"I couldn't wait. I just got through with my audition and I just had to talk to you."

"What happened? Oh, Griffin, did you get it?" Phoebe was now bouncing on the bed and she felt like she might just fly through the roof. Griffin was so talented as an actor. If anybody deserved to get into a Broadway show, he was the one.

"It sure looks that way," Griffin managed. "I can't believe it! I can't believe I'm going to be an understudy for the lead in a Broadway show. Ahhh!" Griffin let out a victory yell, and they both started to laugh.

"Well, what happened? Tell me everything that happened!"

The phone began to click loudly, and a recording came on, asking that the caller deposit more change. Obviously Griffin was at a pay phone.

"Griffin, give me the number of the phone booth. I'll call you right back," Phoebe said. She quickly memorized the number and dialed him back.

"Griffin Neill, New York actor, speaking," Griffin said in a put-on voice as he answered. Phoebe could hear other voices and bustle in the background.

"Where are you?" Phoebe still had a hard time imagining Griffin in New York City. She had never been there, but she had seen the city a million times in photos and movies. Still, she couldn't picture what it was like to really live there.

"Some little coffee shop on Forty-fourth Street.

I was too excited to wait until I got home to call you. Anyway, this third reading was on the stage. It was in a real Broadway theater. It was all dark except for this one light on the stage, and the five of them — the producer and director and some others — they sat in the first row — a private audition. After I finished reading the scene, they asked me to come down off the stage and talk to them."

"Yes." Phoebe was smiling so hard her face was beginning to ache.

"So" — Griffin paused and took a deep breath "they told me I had done a great job and that I was just what they were looking for! Rehearsals start in two days."

"Oh, Griffin, I'm so happy for you!"

"This is the best day of my life." Griffin lowered his voice. "You know the only thing that's missing."

"What?" Phoebe whispered.

"You."

Phoebe felt her pulse speed up as tears welled up in her eyes. Why did she and Griffin have to be so far apart?

"Phoebe, you still there?"

"Yes."

"So, how are you? What's going on there? Is everything okay?"

"Things are fine." *As fine as they could be without you*, Phoebe thought.

"Listen. I can't stand not seeing you for so long. I have a great idea." Griffin paused at what sounded like a tray of dishes crashing to the floor. He laughed. "New York — boy, it's crazy here. Listen. The people I'm staying with are going out of town next week." Griffin was temporarily renting a room in a big apartment. "Why don't you come up to New York next weekend?"

Phoebe felt her cheeks flush. It was just like Griffin to ask something like that without stopping to think that her parents would never allow it. Griffin's mother didn't seem to care what he did, but her folks were strict. There was no way her mom or dad would okay her going to New York and staying in an apartment with her boyfriend alone. No way.

And yet Phoebe felt she just *had* to go. Thinking about seeing Griffin again made her feel so full and happy. Not a day went by that she didn't hurt from missing him. Also, next weekend was homecoming, the time she would be the most reminded of Brad. What could be better than to spend homecoming weekend away with Griffin.

"That would be great. But what about my parents?"

"Oh," Griffin answered. The issue of parents hadn't occurred to him. "I don't know. All I know is how much I miss you. This is such a great time for me, and I want to share it with you."

Phoebe could hear footsteps in the hall. It was her father home from work.

Phoebe lowered her voice. "I'll try and figure out a way to come. I know I can think of something. We'll talk by next Thursday. Okay?"

"Okay."

"Congratulations!"

"Thanks."

"Well." Phoebe paused. Their conversations

95

always ended this way. They knew they had to get off, but neither could bear to hang up the phone.

"I love you," Griffin whispered urgently.

"I love you, too," Phoebe answered. She put down the receiver as her father walked into the bedroom. "I love you" was a much better way to end the conversation than "good-bye."

Phoebe sat on the bed and watched her balding father hang up his jacket and undo his tie. When he smiled at her, she had to look away. She already felt guilty. She knew that her parents would have a fit if they found out that she was planning to spend the weekend in New York with Griffin. She also knew that nothing was going to stop her. She had made up her mind.

Chapter
11

He was the first person Lisa saw when she got out of her mother's car on Monday morning. It almost seemed that he was waiting just for her.

Peter Lacey was leaning against the flagpole, looking out over the parking lot. He was wearing a heavy fisherman's sweater and black jeans and had Walkman headphones over his ears. With one hand he slapped his thigh in rhythm to the music, and every few seconds he mouthed some of the words to the song. When he saw Lisa get out of the car, he pushed the earphones down around his neck and waved energetically. He *was* waiting for her.

Lisa found herself running to meet him. It was a lovely fall day, sunny but brisk. When she got close to Peter, she saw a wonderful look of expectation in his eyes.

"Hi," she said breathlessly.

"Hi."

They stood and grinned at each other.

"How was your weekend?" Lisa asked. It seemed like years since he had visited the rink. Lisa looked away with embarrassment when she realized it had only been two days. She had thought about him so much over the weekend.

"My weekend was great." Peter smiled. "How about yours?"

"Great, too!" Lisa laughed.

"You skated all weekend and you had a really good time. Right?" Peter had a very mischievous look in his eye.

"Yeah. Actually I did. How did you know?"

Peter stuck his hands in his pockets and twisted his foot like a playful little kid. "I watched you," he admitted finally.

"What!"

"Well, not all weekend. Just twice. I sort of snuck in and checked up on you. I stayed in the doorway, so I guess you didn't see me."

"Why didn't you come over and talk to me?"

"You looked like you were having too good a time. I didn't want to break your flow."

Lisa let her stuffed practice bag fall to the concrete and lifted her hands. She was laughing again. "I don't believe this!"

Peter shrugged and laughed, too. "Well, don't worry, I'm not a peeper or anything. I didn't want to distract you; you looked like you were really having fun."

Lisa pushed up the sleeves of her homemade sweater. Her hair was still in pigtails from her morning practice, and the ends rested against her shoulders. She had enjoyed her skating so much that morning that she hadn't left the rink in time to redo her hair.

She had decided to take Peter's advice to heart over the weekend. *Just for the love of it*, she had told herself. She had let herself joke and clown, and she knew that she had never skated better, or had so much fun. She had found the joy again. She hoped she would be able to feel as free when Coach Bielman watched her.

"You know, this afternoon is when I skate for Bielman."

"I wouldn't forget that." Peter smiled. Taking a step toward her, he unhooked the tape player from his belt and put it in her hand. Reaching up, he lightly touched her hair and slipped his earphones over her head.

Lisa looked up at him. She came up to the bottom of his chin. Kids were racing past on the way to first period, but Lisa hardly saw them.

"Why are you giving me your Walkman?"

"A good luck charm. I made a tape especially for you." Peter patted the tape player. "A few songs that I thought would remind you to hang loose, have a good time. You can listen while you're getting ready."

Lisa looked down at the Walkman. Peter actually cared enough about her and her skating to make a tape for her! She felt as if she were bathed in light, as if there were a glowing halo around her body. Without thinking, she reached up, put her arms around Peter's neck, and hugged him. She wanted to thank him and this seemed the most natural way to do it. Peter's sweater was thick and rough, but his neck was very smooth.

"Thank you." She let go, but Peter held on to her hands.

"What time is your tryout for the coach?"

"I'm leaving right after third period. Bielman will be at the rink all afternoon. He's seeing some little kids, too. I'm not sure when I'll be on."

"I'll come and watch as soon as I get out of school." Peter hesitated. "I mean, if you want me to."

At that moment Peter was the one person she did want to come and watch her. Lisa nodded her head in one definite, positive gesture.

"Okay, I'll get there as soon as I can. I promise."

The first-period bell rang, and both Peter and Lisa realized that they were late. They started to go in opposite directions but immediately came back together.

"Good luck," Peter said. "Remember . . ." He paused and put his hand over his heart. Lisa knew just what he meant. ". . . skate for the love of it."

"See you later," Lisa said, backing away slightly.

Peter hesitated, and for a moment they just smiled at each other. Finally, he turned away and began to walk quickly toward his class. Lisa stood and watched him until he was completely out of view.

Phoebe was flying. She had dialed Chris's number five times the night before, but the Austin line had been busy. Now she was trying to catch her at the morning break. Maybe Chris had an idea of how she could get away and see Griffin over

100

homecoming weekend. Maybe Chris would be willing to cover for her.

"Chris!" Phoebe yelled across the quad. Chris was deep in conversation with Ted. Their heads were close together, and his arms were resting on her shoulders. Just seeing them together made Phoebe miss Griffin even more. Phoebe had to yell three times before Chris heard.

Chris looked up and waved. Ted leaned in for one more word before nodding to Phoebe and making a quick exit. Chris stood still in the middle of the quad, lines of tension tightening her all-American face. She had her hands in the pockets of her gray wool blazer.

"Chris, I called you about a million times last night, but I couldn't get through," Phoebe panted. She was dying to tell Chris about Griffin's success.

Chris turned to her with a preoccupied look. "Brenda was on with her old counselor from the halfway house. I think they talked until really late." She looked down at her watch and then over in the direction of the radio station. Her princess interview was in another two hours.

Phoebe put her hand on Chris's arm to get her attention. "Chris, you know who was on the phone when you left yesterday? Griffin!" She quickly filled Chris in on Griffin's wonderful turn of luck.

Chris suddenly began to listen. "That's fantastic. I don't believe it. A Broadway play!"

"I know." Phoebe paused and took a deep breath. "So, anyway . . ." she hesitated, "Griffin asked me if I could come up to New York and stay with him this weekend; you know, over homecoming." Chris looked at her with a startled expression. Phoebe plowed ahead. "I could just take the train up on Saturday morning and come back Sunday. But of course my parents would never let me stay over, so I, um, thought maybe I could say that I was sleeping over at your house...."

Chris responded with a look of instant disapproval.

"Just think about it, Chris. It would work out fine." Phoebe knew she was treading on dangerous ground with her best friend. Chris didn't like breaking rules. Even though she was more easygoing than she used to be, something like this was pushing Chris's limits.

"Well?" Phoebe asked.

Chris let loose with a huge puff of air, as if another weight had just been placed on her shoulders. "Phoebe, I can't decide right now. There're too many other things on my mind. I know how much you want to see Griffin. I'm just not sure that I can lie for you."

Phoebe jumped in. "I understand. Just think about it and let me know. Okay?"

Chris nodded and looked down at the ground. Without saying good-bye, she grabbed her books off the bench and left Phoebe standing alone in the middle of the grassy quad.

Phoebe stuck her hands in her jeans pockets. She knew that she shouldn't have asked Chris to lie for her, that it would make Chris feel pulled between her sense of friendship and her principles. But Phoebe felt out of control. All she could think of was that she had to see Griffin, and she didn't care what she had to do to make it happen.

"Oh, Janie, life is great, isn't it?" Peter grinned as he sailed into the radio station. It was noontime. Peter grabbed Janie's arms and began waltzing her around.

Janie had never seen Peter in such a good mood. He was humming some corny old song and guiding her toward the studio in an old-fashioned tango. Even though he was obviously giddy, he guided her with care and gentleness, and Janie had never felt so graceful. She was very aware of his hand against the small of her back and of the fact that she was most certainly blushing.

"You are a most beautiful dancer, Miss Barstow," Peter teased as he bent her down in an exaggerated dip.

Janie shrieked involuntarily. She hadn't meant to make such a loud sound, but having Peter so close to her made it impossible to stay calm. The strap of her corduroy jumper slipped off her shoulder.

She wondered why Peter was being so warm toward her. Of course, he was always nice to her, always considerate and kind. But today he was acting differently than usual. He was very happy about something. Janie hoped that his mood would hold.

Peter let go of Janie's waist and began a jitterbug instead. Lightly grasping her hands, he playfully twisted and hopped. For a second Janie couldn't resist fantasizing that she and Peter were dancing together at homecoming.

Janie's dream was interrupted when she noticed someone in the doorway. She might have been standing there for some time, watching Peter and Janie dancing together. It was Laurie Bennington.

Peter didn't let Laurie puncture his high spirits. He stopped dancing and bowed to Janie. "Thank you, Madam," he clowned.

Janie curtsied awkwardly and giggled. Laurie Bennington was still staring at them, but now she had a slight smile on her face.

"Are you going to do your radio show or just dance the lunch period away?" Laurie said mildly. She leaned against the door frame and untied the lush knit scarf that hung around her neck.

"I'm ready, Laurie dearest," Peter sang happily, and with a huge smile he walked into the control booth.

Laurie stayed in the doorway and watched Peter disappear. She looked back at Janie. "You two certainly have a good time together, don't you?"

Janie looked down at the ground, making little circles with the toe of her loafer. She was surprised at the tone of Laurie's voice. It was almost friendly. But Laurie's hint that there might be anything between her and Peter made Janie very embarrassed. There was something between them, sure. Unfortunately, it was totally one-sided. Laurie still stood in the doorway and smiled.

Janie heard someone rounding the corner and

coming toward the station. A second later, Chris Austin rushed into the room. When she saw Laurie Bennington, she froze in her tracks.

Janie watched the two girls size each other up. Janie envied both of them their looks, yet Chris's beauty was much more understated and natural. In her pleated plaid skirt and blazer, she was a classically dressed girl who happened to have a lovely face and long blonde hair. Laurie, whose looks were flashier and more obvious, was dressed in a chic black jump suit with wide shoulders and a low neckline. It was an outfit calculated to impress and intimidate. But it was obvious that it had no effect on Chris.

The smile disappeared from Laurie's face. "Have a good interview, Austin," she said, meaning just the opposite. She started to leave.

Chris stopped her. "I suggest you listen to it, Laurie. I plan to say some things that you should hear."

"Oh, really. You know, I wouldn't even bother with an interview if I were you. Ever since Lisa Chang came into the picture everybody's lost interest in voting for you." Laurie tapped her long, manicured fingernails against the wall. Janie continued to stare at the tiled floor and listen.

"Laurie" — Chris sounded as if she was trying to stay calm — "Lisa has nothing to do with this, and you know it."

"Really? It seems to me that Lisa has you pretty upset. But then Lisa is more popular and a better candidate, so I can see how you'd feel pretty threatened."

"You know what I mean, Laurie," Chris continued with a real edge to her voice.

"All I know is that you thought you had the race sewn up until Lisa Chang decided to run. . . ."

"You mean until you decided to make her run," interrupted Chris.

"You said that, not me. Anyway, just because you're jealous of Lisa. . . ." With that, Laurie turned dramatically, tossed the end of her scarf over her shoulder, and marched away.

Chris looked at Janie and shook her head with pure disgust.

Janie felt for Chris. Chris was a good person. She never treated Janie like a nothing the way Laurie did.

"Chris," Janie said softly, "it's time for you to go in and do your interview."

Chris was still staring at the place where Laurie had stood. Her face looked stern, and her mouth was tight and angry. There wasn't much that Janie was sure of, but there was one thing she did know. The way Chris looked right now, she was in no shape to give a radio interview. No shape at all.

Chapter
12

"Hi there, Cardinals. Peter Lacey here on WKND. And what a great day it is! Let's start off this perfect afternoon with some perfect rock 'n' roll. Here he is, your favorite and mine, the boss himself, Bruce Springsteen!"

Lisa giggled happily as she plopped down on the locker room bench. The songs that Peter had recorded for her had made her feel silly and loose. But at noon she'd realized that his Walkman could also be used as a radio. On a hunch she pushed the switch and set the dial on WKND. Amazingly, the station was coming through as clearly as Peter's tape.

Lisa adjusted the earphones and finished unlacing and pulling off her skates. She had to change from her practice clothes into the performance outfit that was hanging on the locker next to hers. After putting on a plain royal blue skating dress, she carefully examined the edges of her skate blades and listened to Peter's lively, charming voice. Just the sound of it was like a warm spray over her body. Hearing his show was the perfect psychological warmup for the afternoon ahead.

"I'm back, Cardinals. It's another big day here on WKND. Sitting at my side is the lovely Chris Austin, candidate for junior homecoming princess, and we are going to find out just what kind of candidate she is," Peter's voice explained happily.

"Hello." Chris sounded cautious.

"So let's see here, Chris Austin. The list of your accomplishments is most impressive. Head of the honor society, debate, tennis, and you are a special supporter of the football team," Peter teased, referring to Ted's position as quarterback. He laughed, and Lisa laughed, too.

Strangely, there was no response from Chris. Lisa heard what sounded like a rustling, as if Chris was shifting in her chair. It must be the reception, Lisa thought. She knew Chris would give a good interview. Lisa didn't expect to win and wasn't jealous of Chris's chances. For Lisa, being included was what mattered most.

Suddenly Chris's voice came over the headphones. Only it didn't sound like the normal Chris. The voice was tight and clipped.

"Peter," Chris said angrily, "I have something to say that is very important. There is someone else who has been spreading malicious gossip on this radio station about someone very close to me. It's totally unfair, and the person that she's hurting has nothing to do with the homecoming contest."

Lisa was confused. This was an interview for homecoming princess, so why was Chris talking about something that she herself admitted had nothing to do with the race? It sounded weird.

Peter seemed to be thinking the same thing. "Then maybe we should go on and talk about things that do have to do with homecoming. Now, would you tell. . . ."

Chris ignored him. "Peter, it's all tied together. Oh, there's no reason not to use names. Laurie Bennington certainly doesn't have any scruples about that. She has a grudge against me and is trying to do anything she can to get me to drop out of the race, whether it be telling lies about my stepsister or using Lisa Chang to defeat girls who really deserve to win."

Lisa felt a jolt go through her. What was going on? What did Chris mean about Laurie using her?

Peter broke in. "Lisa is just another candidate. If anything weird is going on, I'm sure Lisa has no part in it."

Chris's voice seemed to acknowledge that she knew she had gone too far. "I'm not trying to say anything against Lisa. She's a special person. But it's Laurie who is trying to make a joke out of this contest. It's just that someone like Lisa, who's never had time to do anything for the school, is hardly the person you honor to represent your class, no matter how nice she may be. I'm not saying that I'm the person either. All the other girls who are running have been involved in after-school events and have worked to make Kennedy a better place. But Laurie — by trying to get everybody to vote for Lisa just because she wants me to lose — hurts all the other candidates, too."

Lisa stopped relacing her skates and sat on the bench like a statue. She felt as if she had just had the wind knocked out of her. From the beginning, she'd felt that there was something not right about her nomination. She had also sensed that Laurie was not a good person, not someone to be trusted. But Lisa had so wanted to be part of homecoming, she had let herself be used. Her nomination had nothing to do with her own merits. Laurie had simply been using her to settle some vendetta with Chris. It was stupid of her to think that after all this time her classmates would just accept her and include her in their most honored activities. She was an outsider, and she should have stayed that way.

Peter was now trying to guide the interview back to Chris's accomplishments and qualifications, but Chris was still going on about Laurie and how it all wasn't fair. Lisa angrily pulled the earphones off her head and tossed them onto the rubber matting. She should never have tried to get more involved in school. She wondered if Peter considered her a fool for letting Laurie use her.

At that moment her mother appeared in the doorway. "Lisa, Coach Bielman is here. He'd like to see your short program as soon as you are ready. Good luck, darling."

110

Lisa looked up sharply. Bielman was out there! She had to wipe all this out of her mind and concentrate on her skating. She continued to lace up her skates and mouthed her special good luck chant as she pulled the long laces across the hooks. But it was no use. As soon as she'd finished tying the laces she started thinking about the interview again. She felt so used! What if everyone at school thought that she had wanted to help Laurie defeat Chris? Maybe they all thought that she was Laurie's good friend. Now Lisa remembered back to Peter's first interview, some of his first comments. No wonder he had tried to ruin her chances. He knew she didn't deserve to run, too.

Stop thinking about it! Concentrate on your short program!

Lisa angrily slipped on her blade guards and walked out into the rink. She tried to go over her routine in her head, but her thoughts were bouncing around like a Ping-Pong ball. Perhaps it was better that she had to give up her social life. Maybe it was good that skating was the only thing in her life, that was how it was meant to be.

Suddenly, more than ever, it became very important that she not make any mistakes in her short program. Bielman had to let her train in Colorado. Then she could leave Rose Hill. Sure she would miss Peter, but at least she could get away from this awful mess.

Lisa approached the edge of the ice and looked up into the stands. Of course Peter wasn't there. It was too early, he would still be in class. And maybe he had changed his mind. Maybe after

Chris's interview he didn't want the kids at school to know that he liked the girl who let herself be used by Laurie Bennington.

Lisa did spot Coach Bielman. He was sitting casually in the center of the bleachers, chatting with her mother. Although he was a pudgy, ordinary-looking man, Lisa knew he was the toughest skating coach in the world. Just seeing his relaxed posture and silly red stocking-cap made her even more nervous. She had to skate her best. Bielman wouldn't be fooled by anything less.

With a slight wave, the coach let Lisa know that he was ready. Lisa slipped off her skate guards and stroked out to the center of the rink. She tried to clear her mind, but all she could think of was how awful it would be if she failed. If Bielman didn't take her, she would probably not go much further with her skating. She would still be an outsider at school. She would have nothing.

Lisa was to do her short program first. It was a two-minute freestyle routine that had to include seven different difficult jumps, leaps, and spins. It was a test of a skater's proficiency. The short program was usually a strong one for Lisa, as the emphasis was on properly executing each of the moves. Still, as Lisa waited for her music to begin, she felt incredibly nervous and distracted.

The echoey music began. It was a short selection from *West Side Story*. Lisa went into her first double-jump combination without any problem. But as soon as she came out of it, she began to worry about hitting the next one. *Don't blow it,*

Lisa. Don't blow it, she repeated to herself. Her legs flew up over the ice and she came back down abruptly. Not a great landing, but at least no fall. She kept moving.

But she was in trouble. Anytime she worried about falling she knew she was thinking about the wrong thing. The one sure way to fall was to worry about it. Now she was going from move to move just hoping to get through each one without a mistake. She was not tying the moves together or projecting anything to the audience. The two minutes seemed like two hours.

When Lisa finally stood in her final pose she couldn't have felt less triumphant. She had completed her routine without any big mistakes, and yet she knew exactly how she had done. She'd blown her chances with Coach Bielman again.

Not able to look her mother or Bielman in the face, Lisa quickly left the ice and retreated to the locker room. "Ugh," she whispered to herself. "That was so bad. . . ."

She wrapped herself in the thick blue sweater her mom had knitted for her. She felt sick. A very young girl was on her way out to skate for Bielman, and Lisa didn't even wish her luck.

A few minutes later there was a knock at the locker room door. Lisa shouted that she was decent and looked up to see Mr. Helde sit down next to her. Her mother was standing silently behind him. Helde was nervously tugging at his mustache, and his face looked very old and worn.

"Is your ankle bothering you?" Mr. Helde asked in an unsure voice.

"That's not it," Lisa answered disgustedly. "I just didn't skate very well. I'm sorry."

The old man put his arm around her. "Did I say that?" he asked with a forced joviality. "I just asked about your ankle. You did just fine. Coach Bielman will see your long program after he's seen all the children and talked to their parents. That gives you a while to relax and have some cocoa. When it's time for your long program, just remember to listen to the music. Let your movements flow. Remember, you begin when the music starts and you don't end until it is over. It's one long statement. Ya?"

Lisa nodded and tried to smile. She knew that Mr. Helde would never tell her she had done badly when she had to get out on the ice again that day. He would give her support and try to help get her back on course. It wouldn't be until later that he'd let her know how poorly she'd really done.

Her mother stepped in and gave her a hug. "I love you, Lisa, and I'm very proud of you," she said with a tight smile. That made Lisa feel even worse about disappointing her. Mr. Helde and her mom walked back out to the rink.

The younger skaters and their mothers wandered in and out of the dressing room. Bielman was obviously checking out the latest crop of future champions on his visit east. One tiny dark-haired child slammed the locker shut and practically ran out to the rink. The little girl was so excited to get out on the ice that she practically tripped over her skates. That was how Lisa had felt all weekend. And how she should have felt today. But no. Things hadn't worked out. How could they? She was trapped in the circle of doubt and defeat again.

Lisa went out to the edge of the bleachers and watched the children glide, wobble, spin, and fall for Coach Bielman. But most of it was a blur. As the time went by, she thought more and more about Peter. She was worried that he had changed his mind about her. When she looked at her watch and saw that it was three-thirty, she knew her fears had come true. School had been let out forty minutes ago. If Peter were coming he would have been there already.

At three-forty Lisa went out to the lobby to warm up again. There was still no sign of Peter; no phone call, no note. He had given up on her. Lisa felt a burning at the back of her eyes and a tightness in her throat. She tried to keep going with her exercises, but she was too distracted and weary.

Leaning over the Dutch door that led to Mr. Helde's office, she looked at an old picture of herself that was hanging over his desk. In it she was ten years old, wearing a glittery leotard and skating skirt and holding her first trophy. The smile on her face was uncomplicated and full. That was before she had known what it was to be so disappointed. Before she had understood what it meant to feel struck and hurt.

Instead of going back to her exercises, Lisa leaned with her back to the wall and stared out the front door. A single tear rolled silently down her cheek.

Chapter 13

"Come on!" yelled Peter as he slammed his fist against the metal dashboard of his old Volkswagen. He had thought of everything — at least, he thought he'd thought of everything. Above all else, he wanted to make sure that he would get to the ice rink in time to see Lisa skate for Coach Bielman. He had run out of seventh period physics before the bell had rung. He had raced across the parking lot and barely missed being sideswiped by Marisa Jones on a motor scooter. He had risked getting a ticket at the speed trap near Templeton Boulevard and had floored it just about the whole way. But now, at the top of Frederick Avenue, almost two miles from the Capitol Rink, Peter's "bug" was beginning to bug out.

Peter desperately urged it on. Come on! Just two more miles! It was then than Peter looked at the gas gauge. Empty! He had forgotten to put gas in the tank. How incredibly stupid! With all his preoccupation with Lisa and Laurie, and Chris and everything else, he had neglected to do something just that simple!

There was no alternative but to continue by foot. Peter quickly pushed the old bug onto the dirt shoulder, locked the doors, and began to run.

As his feet pounded against the ground, he thought back to Chris and her interview. He still felt a wave of surprise as he remembered what had happened. Chris had really lit into Laurie — blazed away with both guns. And even though Chris was right, he was very glad that Lisa hadn't been at school to hear the interview. There was no way he wanted Lisa hurt.

Lisa was on her way back into the rink when she heard a strong knock on the double glass doors. Slowly she turned, and when she saw Peter through the window, she felt all her listlessness disappear and a surge of energy return to her limbs. He hadn't given up on her after all!

She quickly opened the door. Peter was panting as if *he* had just finished a skating routine himself.

"You made it," Lisa said, her chest heaving.

"Finally," Peter panted.

He wiped his damp forehead with the cuff of his bomber jacket. He was still huffing as he whipped off his jacket.

"I'm really glad you're here," Lisa said immediately.

"I almost didn't make it."

"I understand."

"You do?" Peter looked pretty confused.

"I knew you'd have weird feelings about being with me after your show."

"What?" Peter was puzzled.

Lisa wanted to get it out in the open. "After the interview with Chris. I mean, now everybody knows how I let myself be used by Laurie."

"Wait a minute. Lisa, what are you talking about? You mean you heard Chris's interview?"

Lisa nodded.

"But you were here at the rink, weren't you?"

"I listened on your Walkman."

Peter slumped against the wall. "Oh, man. I never thought of that. I'm sorry." Peter ran his hand through his hair. "Wait a second. You mean you thought I might not come because of that interview? I know I wasn't such a nice guy the first time we met, but do you think I'm a total jerk?"

There was a very indignant look in his eyes. Now Lisa was confused and unable to answer.

"Lisa, do you think I would care about something dumb like that? I knew about Laurie's scheme a long time ago."

"I know. I just thought that now that your whole crowd knew it — then when you were late. I don't know." Lisa looked away, too embarrassed to meet Peter's gaze.

"You finally stopped worrying about your skating, so you decided to worry about something else. Nobody blames you for this junk with Laurie. Especially not me. Listen, after the interview, Chris felt even worse than you do. She's really embarrassed." He paused and smiled

118

slightly. "You really want to know why I'm late?"

"Why?"

"Because I was too dumb to fill up my own gas tank."

"What?"

"Yeah." Peter gave a sheepish look. "I ran all the way from the top of Frederick."

"You did?"

"I sure did."

Lisa shook her head and began to laugh. Suddenly it all seemed very silly. Peter started to laugh, too, and Lisa felt his arm drape over her shoulder. She leaned her head toward him and could feel his muscular shoulder under the soft cotton of his faded shirt.

"Owww," Peter complained suddenly, still laughing. Lisa had stepped on his foot with her skate. They laughed harder, letting the giggling build to a silly pitch.

"We make a great pair," Lisa panted. "I'm a paranoid klutz, and you can't even remember that cars run on gas."

The laughing felt so good. It was as if all that tension and worry was being laughed out. Lisa was beginning to wonder just why she had let herself get so upset in the first place.

A tiny girl pushed open the door to the foyer. She was wearing a pink skating skirt and a sweat shirt that said "Skating Moves Me." Shyly, she looked first at Lisa and then at Peter.

"Miss Chang," the little girl said politely. She had a striped ribbon around her curly blond ponytail.

Lisa looked at Peter and stifled another

laugh. "Yes," Lisa answered, bending to meet the girl's eye.

"It's your turn now." The girl started to go but turned to add, "I get to watch." Her voice was filled with pride. She smiled and disappeared back into the rink.

Peter put his hands on Lisa's shoulders so she was facing him. He just put his hand to his heart in the gesture they had planned that morning. "Skate because you love it. And for that little kid, too," he said.

Lisa looked into Peter's green eyes. They were filled with support and warmth. She turned, took a big breath, and pushed open the glass door that led to the rink. There was no one on the ice, and Bielman was sitting in the middle of the bleachers. Scattered across the rows of benches were six or seven little girls and boys and their parents.

Lisa headed straight onto the ice and began stroking in a circle, going over her long routine in her head. She was marking some of the movements with her arms and humming her music to herself.

The long routine was the most important part of any skating competition. In it Lisa had four minutes to do a choreographed routine that was supposed to show off her skill and expressiveness. Athletic ability and technique were Lisa's strengths, but the elements of artistry and expression had been her weaknesses. And those were just the elements that counted the most in the long routine.

Lisa gave Mr. Helde the sign that she was

ready for her music. She skated into the middle of the rink and bent over in her starting position.

The first move of the routine was for Lisa to slowly uncurl until at last her face was exposed to the audience. This slow beginning was for dramatic effect and was meant to contrast with the flashier jumps and spins that came later.

Lisa heard the music begin. Gershwin's "Rhapsody in Blue." Slowly she let herself be guided by the sound. As she lifted her face for the first time, she saw Peter smiling at her. He was sitting in the top row and still had his hand over his heart. Just looking at his smile made Lisa want to share with everyone the way she felt. As if to let Peter know that she understood his message, Lisa threw back her head and began to move.

The motion did something to Lisa. It was as if she suddenly understood the power of a gesture, a single movement. If she wanted to communicate with the people in the audience — and with Peter — she could do it. Suddenly every movement of her routine had a new meaning. When she lifted her arm she was reaching to Peter; when she spun and leapt away she was teasing and playing and asking him to follow her.

For the first time she understood what she was doing. She was asking the audience to come and be a part of her skating so that she wouldn't be so alone. The faster she spun, the more they understood and the closer they were. As she came to the end of her routine it was as if she were saying good-bye, letting them know she didn't really want to leave them, but the time had run

121

out. There was a loud chord, and Lisa stopped in a sudden freeze. She lifted her face and would have laughed, except there were two tiny tears rolling down her face. It was over.

The little girl in the "Skating Moves Me" shirt stood up and cheered. Peter joined her, followed by Lisa's mother and a few of the other children. Lisa slowly skated to the edge of the ice and leaned on the railing.

Mr. Helde was the first to reach her.

"Lisa, that was so good! At last you understand what I say to you! Oh, that is so good!" He hugged her over the barrier. She would never have told her beloved old teacher that it was nothing he had said to her, but something she had learned on her own.

After Mr. Helde came her mother. Mrs. Chang gave her daughter a kiss and told her tearily what a wonderful job she had done. Waiting behind Mrs. Chang was a stern-faced Coach Bielman.

Bielman waited for Mrs. Chang to leave before he began to speak. "You've improved since the last time I saw you. Your short program was weak, but your long routine was quite impressive."

Lisa was glued to his every word, his every gesture. He was lifting a page on his clipboard and writing underneath. Finally he raised his head. "I can tell your ankle's injured," he said gruffly. "No training for the next week at least, and see this physical therapist."

He tore a square of paper off and handed it to her. "Do you understand? One week off the ice. Give that ankle a chance to rest." Bielman paused and patted her on the hand. "I'll call you

122

sometime soon and let you know my decision."

Bielman gave her a slight wave and walked straight out of the rink. Lisa watched him go. He never looked back. She felt the excitement building inside of her. The coach hadn't said yes, but he certainly hadn't said no. Bielman had said that she'd improved. Whether he took her or not, she had done well.

Lisa looked up, hoping to see Peter. There he was, sitting in the same place. He was gazing down at her. He had obviously been waiting for her to finish talking to Bielman and did not move when she caught his eye. He continued to sit with his chin in his hands and stare down at her.

Lisa quickly slipped on her skate guards and stepped off the ice. Carefully, she took hold of the stair rail and began to climb the wooden steps toward the top of the bleachers. Peter never took his eyes off her as she got nearer and nearer. When she finally approached his row, he stood up to meet her. Before Lisa knew it, he had wrapped his arms around her in a giant hug. She felt the fine ends of his hair brush against her cheek and her mouth.

Peter's arms slid down around her waist and Lisa pulled back slightly to look into his face. His eyes were filled with such love that Lisa felt as if she were sunning herself in it. Peter moved in closer, and Lisa let her eyes close. She felt her heart beating quickly. Her arms were up around Peter's neck, and she could feel that his heart was pounding, too. Peter began to kiss her. The kiss was long and gentle, and all Lisa knew was that she had never felt anything like it before.

When Peter and Lisa heard the high-pitched giggling, they finally let each other go. Three small girls were huddled at the bottom of the stands and staring up at them mischievously. Peter waved at them, and the girls giggled even more loudly before running off toward the locker room.

"Nice to know we're entertaining them," Peter joked. He looked a little embarrassed.

"They're just jealous." Lisa beamed. She took Peter's hands and looked down at the ice. His hands were warm and strong. Lisa felt as if she could have floated right across the rink. "I think I took your advice when I was down there. At least I felt like I did." She looked into Peter's face to see if he agreed.

Peter gave an amazed laugh. "My advice? What you did out there had nothing to do with me. That was pure you, and it was incredible! If that guy doesn't take you, he's got a loose transistor." They both laughed.

Lisa felt a chill of cold, and Peter immediately put his arm around her. She leaned her cheek against his hand. "I could feel it. I really did. And I had a great time. I wasn't alone out there!"

"You sure weren't. I was more nervous than you were." Peter turned to face her and ran his hand along the side of her face. "It was really beautiful," he said seriously. He looked away with a hint of self-consciousness. "Look, I know you have to keep on a tough schedule and all, but this is a special night. What do you say we go out and celebrate? The crowd is going to the

Sub Shop after today's pep rally. Do you think you could go?"

Lisa closed her eyes and took a deep breath. Two hours ago that would have been the last thing she wanted to do. But something had changed. If she extended herself to her friends — as she had to the audience — they would respond in kind. And Peter . . . she knew there was no turning away from him now. The feeling she had inside was so huge that she would have to follow it.

"Bielman gave me strict orders. . . ."

"I know," Peter interrupted sadly.

"Wait, I'm not finished. Bielman gave me orders not to do any skating for one week so my ankle can get better. To me that sounds like I can actually go."

Peter looked at her with surprise and pleasure. "Honest? You really can?"

"Just give me ten minutes to change." Lisa grinned. She started to leave but quickly turned back to him. "You know something? I can't remember the last time I went out with old friends and people I cared about."

"That's okay," Peter bantered back. "I can't remember the last time I went out with one girl I really cared about."

They continued to stand there, smiling at each other.

"Hey, hurry up and change," Peter teased happily, glancing at his watch, "you have nine and a half minutes left."

Chapter
14

Lisa dressed in exactly ten minutes. She was that excited. In fact, she was flying so high that she was way ahead of Peter and had to wait for him while her mom took him to get gas. Finally Peter's Volkswagen pulled up in front of the door, and Lisa ran out before he had a chance to come inside and get her. She hopped into the front seat, and Peter turned down the song that was playing on his tape deck. He leaned toward her and tousled her hair.

"You look great," he said softly.

"I do?" Lisa was wearing a combination of practice and street clothes: jeans, pink leg warmers, white leotard, patterned sweater vest, and her homemade cardigan. She decided she liked this half-and-half way of dressing.

"You do. Take my word for it."

Peter let out the clutch and backed out of the parking lot.

"The car's moving again, huh?"

Peter shrugged and tapped the dashboard with his fist. "Yeah," he said. "It was pretty embarrassing to meet your mom that way. 'Hi. I'm Peter. I don't know that cars need gas.'" He reached over and pushed the gearshift. "Anyway, your mom's really proud of you. She said it doesn't matter if Bielman takes you or not, because you did your best."

Lisa leaned against the window. She knew her mom was right.

"It's funny, whenever I've had times I didn't think I wanted to skate anymore, my mom has always made me stick with it. She talks about how you have to sacrifice something to do anything really special. After today, even if Bielman doesn't take me, I think I understand what she means. Something happened out there on the ice. Partly it was because of you, partly all the years of work. But that feeling I got out there when I skated my long program, it made all the sacrifices worth it." Lisa nodded, almost to herself. It was all becoming clearer to her, and she knew that if anyone could understand, it was Peter. "You know, it's weird. In order to do something really well I guess you sometimes have to set yourself apart from other people."

"Yeah. Like me and the radio station. 'Cause I do the radio show, I can't eat lunch with my friends. So I have to give that up."

"Right."

"But you know, Lis, you can't totally block out other people —"

Lisa interrupted, — or you'll feel lonely and

127

cut off. Yeah. You know what I also think?"

"What?" Peter stopped at a red light and turned to face her.

"That if you get too cut off, then you can't do your best at whatever it is you're cutting yourself off to do." Lisa laughed.

Peter nodded excitedly and began to snap his fingers to the radio. "Sure! It's like a really good stereo. This may sound off the wall, but . . . you have to read all these books and learn about electronics and all that to know how to build a stereo. But then you have to spend time with people, sort of learning about life and feeling stuff. Because if you don't, it won't matter how great the stereo is, you won't appreciate the music." Peter paused and gave her a funny smile as he pulled into the parking lot of the Mill Creek Shopping Mall. "Did you get that?"

Lisa laughed and pulled at her leg warmers. "Believe it or not, I did." It was so easy to talk to Peter. Once their initial misunderstanding had been cleared up, they had totally understood each other. It was amazing how much they really had in common.

A long station wagon was pulling out of a prime spot right in front of the sub shop door. Peter waited for it to pull away. As the wagon swung back, Lisa recognized Phoebe Hall's thick mane of wavy red hair. Phoebe saw Lisa at the same time and stuck her head out the window to say hello.

"Hi!!!" Phoebe yelled excitedly.

Lisa leaned across Peter and said hello. Phoebe

looked back and forth between Lisa and Peter. Peter leaned close to Lisa and put his arm around her. Phoebe gave Lisa a knowing smile.

"How are you, Lisa?" Phoebe leaned her elbows on the inside of her open car window. "It's great to see you. How did you manage to get out of practice?"

Lisa explained how she had to lay off training because of her ankle. She also told Phoebe about Coach Bielman. At the mention of possibly going away to Colorado, Phoebe gave Lisa a hard look.

"Well, good luck." Phoebe bit down on her lower lip.

Lisa got the feeling that her possible move had reminded Phoebe of Griffin. Just as he and Phoebe had fallen in love, Griffin had left for New York. Phoebe obviously saw a parallel to Lisa's situation.

It wasn't that long ago that Phoebe had come to Lisa for sympathy and advice about Griffin. Lisa smiled as she remembered how she'd told Phoebe she doubted she would ever fall in love. How quickly things had changed. As if she knew what Lisa was thinking, Phoebe raised her head and gave a slow nod.

"Oh, Lisa," Phoebe added, "Chris is inside, and I know she wants to talk to you."

Peter and Lisa looked at each other. With an embarrassed wave, Phoebe drove out of the parking lot.

Peter watched the station wagon disappear and looked back at Lisa. He cocked his head as if to say it would be interesting to hear what Chris had to say. "I hope you like submarine sandwiches. The ones here are outrageous," he said with a smile. "Shall we go inside?"

Peter pushed open the thick-timbered restaurant door and instantly there was a blast of music and the sound of dozens of voices all busily chatting away.

Lisa stopped in the entryway. It was a long, crowded room filled with picnic-style tables and benches. An old motorcycle hung on one wall, and there were Kennedy pennants draped from the heavy rafters. The smell of salami and tomatoes filled the crowded room. In the back, Lisa saw an antique jukebox nestled between a wooden Indian and a stuffed polar bear.

"Peter!"

Woody Webster's voice pierced through the music and the noise. He climbed over a wooden bench, kicking up a mound of sawdust. One hand was hooked in his red suspenders, and in the other he held a huge sandwich.

Peter and Lisa made their way over. "Woody, you know Lisa, don't you?"

Woody smiled and caught a piece of salami that was sliding out of his sub. "Yeah. I mean, we've met. Phoebe took me to see you skate in some competition about three years ago. You were shorter then," Woody teased. "Hey, guys, you should have come to the pep rally. It was a classic. I got everybody into a real frenzy with my cheers. 'Course, then I had to calm them back down again because Mr. Zucker thought things were getting out of hand."

Ted Mason waved hello to Lisa and answered

Woody from the far side of a crowded table. "Well, you have to admit, Woody, that the people stamping in the back row were going a little bit overboard. When they picked up that freshman kid and began passing him back and forth like a log. . . ."

"Hey," Woody said, both hands up in protest, "that's an old and time-tested Kennedy ritual. I didn't start that."

Lisa watched as Peter joined in the banter, and three boys kidded each other with a familiarity that came from having spent a lot of time together. It was like a family, and Lisa knew immediately that it was part of what she had been missing. As if he read her mind, Peter pulled her toward him to make sure that she felt included. She stood in front of him and he wound his arms over her shoulders.

It was then that she saw Chris Austin. Chris was walking toward the table, holding two large paper cups. Her blonde hair was swept back in a French braid, and she wore khaki slacks and a pinstriped blouse. Chris started to sit down next to Ted, but she stopped when she saw Lisa.

"Hi," Lisa said evenly. She watched Chris put the drinks down. Both Ted and Peter were watching, too.

"Lisa," Chris began in an embarrassed voice. "I want to talk to you about something. Can we go somewhere for a few minutes?"

"Sure. Peter, I'll be right back."

Lisa followed Chris to a small table next to the counter. As they sat down, Lisa noticed a boy leaning moodily against the other end of the

131

counter. He was staring at his sandwich, his tweed jacket was slung over his shoulder, and from his posture it was obvious that he wanted to be left alone.

"What's the matter with Brad Davidson?" Lisa couldn't help asking. Chris followed Lisa's gaze. "Is he okay?"

Chris sighed nervously. It seemed she was relieved to put off the main topic of their conversation, even if only for a minute. "I think he just needs a few minutes by himself. Phoebe was here, and he got really upset when he saw her. I think he would have left, except that Phoebe felt so weird that she left first. It's awful how Brad can't seem to get over her."

There was a short pause. Lisa continued to watch Brad stare sadly in front of him. At that moment he looked like anything but Kennedy's Ivy League—bound student body president. Lisa felt Chris touch her arm and turned back.

"Listen, what I wanted to say was . . . well, you probably don't know about this, but I did something today on Peter's radio show that. . . ."

"Chris, I heard it," Lisa confessed quickly. This was obviously difficult for Chris, and Lisa didn't want to make it any worse.

Chris closed her eyes in humiliation. "Oh, Lisa, I am so sorry. I have this way of just jumping in when I'm angry and saying things I regret later. It's not one of my best qualities."

"It's okay. Honest."

"I didn't mean to let your name get into it. It really has nothing to do with you. What I did was just as bad as Laurie. I'm sorry."

132

"Chris, I understand. It's okay. In some ways you were right, and it's a good thing that I found out what was going on."

Chris smiled gratefully.

"There is one thing I'm kind of curious about. What ever happened to make Laurie so angry with you and Peter?"

Chris explained what had happened the night of Laurie's party, how Laurie had been after Peter and blamed Chris for her lack of success. Lisa felt an involuntary smile spread across her face at the mention of Laurie's unsuccessful crush. She was beginning to get more of the whole picture.

Chris continued to apologize, but Lisa's mind was racing ahead. She was figuring out just how to remedy the situation.

Just then Peter walked over to join them. He had Brad in tow. It looked as though Peter had had some success at cheering Brad up. The student body president was now at least trying to smile. The boys sat down with Lisa and Chris.

"Did you know that this guy is going to homecoming with Jaws herself. Jaws Bennington," Peter teased. Both Lisa and Chris looked up in surprise.

"Brad, is that true?" Chris asked. She was unable to keep her voice free of her dislike.

Brad looked at her, and that depressed look returned to his face.

"It's okay, Brad. We're just teasing you. If you really have the hots for Bennington, it's none of our business." Peter tilted back in his chair and stuck his hands in the pockets of his black jeans.

133

"Who said I had the hots for her?" Brad said defensively. "I think she's a jerk. It's just that she caught me off guard, and she asked me, and now I'm stuck."

"Sure, Brad," Ted piped up. "That's what Anthony said about Cleopatra." He had stepped in behind Chris a moment before and was tugging on his girl friend's braid.

"No, I mean it."

Lisa could tell from Brad's voice that he really did mean it. She felt sorry for him. His voice sounded so empty and flat. In his state it would be easy for a girl like Laurie to manipulate him. Look how easily Laurie had manipulated her.

Ted tugged again on Chris's hair. "I hope you've finished your talk, because I gotta go home. We're going to go check out the field at Carlton before school tomorrow."

Chris quickly looked at her wristwatch. "I didn't know it was so late. Lisa, I meant what I said. I'm really sorry."

"Don't worry about it."

Chris smiled tentatively, her face relaxing. Then she turned to Brad. "Brad, you want a ride home?"

Brad shrugged. "No, thanks. I'm going to get a ride with Woody later."

"Okay." Chris nodded. "See you in school to-morrow." Ted also said good-bye.

A couple of sub sandwiches and Pepsis later, Peter and Lisa were finally alone again in his Volkswagen. Lisa turned toward him and sat cross-legged on the seat. "Guess you've put up with a lot from Laurie Bennington, huh?" she teased. "Chris explained some things to me. It sounds like Jaws Bennington tried to take a bite out of you, too."

Peter laughed a funny, embarrassed laugh. He ran his hand through his hair as he steered the car toward Lisa's street.

"I never liked her or anything," he said finally, pulling up in front of her white brick house. "I should have figured out that she liked me sooner. I get so wrapped up in the station that sometimes I don't notice stuff like that. Oh, well, it's all over now."

"It sure is," Lisa teased.

"Oh, I get it. Tough girl, huh?" Peter mocked back. He turned on the tape deck and slunk down in his seat. "Hey, baby." He took a puff of an imaginary cigarette.

Lisa slunk down in her small seat and played along. "Yeah, man." The song was soft and melodic. Peter began to snap his fingers.

"So, you having an okay time with me?" Peter asked, nuzzling his head against her shoulder.

Lisa suddenly started to laugh. How could Peter think she was anything but crazy about him? It occurred to her what a day it had been. This was still the same day that she had skated for Bielman. She began to realize that she had finally broken out of that circle. The more she thought about that the more she laughed, and the freer she felt. Yes! She had stepped over the line. And there was no going back now. Peter was staring at her, watching her laugh to herself. Finally she stopped and sat still with a goofy look on her face.

"Okay," Peter said, "I was going to ask you to go to homecoming with me, but since you think I'm so funny maybe I should relieve Brad and take Laurie Bennington instead." He leaned back and looked at her.

"Homecoming?"

"Yeah. You know. Big dance. You wear a fancy dress. I get you some dopey corsage. So, you want to go?"

If Lisa thought she'd used up her quota of emotion that day she proved herself wrong. She was so excited she realized she was slapping the seat and grinning.

"Does that mean yes? It'd better. I don't think I've ever asked anybody on a real date before."

"Under one condition," Lisa answered as Peter pulled her toward him. His wavy hair brushed against her cheek. "After what Chris told me, I've decided to drop out of the princess contest. Do you mind?"

Peter's green eyes told her instantly that he agreed with her decision. "You know something? You are not only a great skater and beautiful, you are also supremely intelligent. But then, of course, you did decide to hang around with me." Peter moved his hand along her shoulder. "There's only one person who's as terrific as you are."

Lisa pulled back, but Peter struggled to keep her close to him. "Oh yeah, who?" she answered playfully.

Peter moved his cheek slowly along hers until he whispered in her ear. "Bruce Springsteen."

Lisa started to laugh again, but Peter stopped

her. This kiss started short and light, but by the time it ended, Lisa could barely remember where she was.

Lisa had missed a lot in the last sixteen years, but she was making up for it fast.

Chapter
15

"Lisa, you look fabulous!" Laurie Bennington shrieked. "That outfit is so hot!"

Lisa looked up from her bicycle lock and smiled to herself. Laurie Bennington was standing over her, wearing a red knit sweater and matching mid-calf skirt. Her yellow boots matched the T-shirt that was under the heavy, oversize sweater. Lisa had seen outfits like that only in expensive shop windows.

In contrast, Lisa was wearing two layered leotards, jeans, and Nikes, with a favorite ski sweater tied around her waist. Needless to say, Laurie was buttering her up again. Only this time, Lisa wasn't going to fall for it.

Actually, Lisa was relieved that Laurie had sought her out so early in the morning. It would save her the trouble of having to find Laurie.

"I'm glad to see you, Laurie." Lisa stood up

and unstrapped her books from the rack on the back of her old bike.

"Did you ride to school?" Laurie said, suddenly unable to hide her disdain. She gave Lisa's rusty three-speed the once-over.

"Well, I'm not doing my morning practice because I hurt my ankle, so I thought it would be good for my legs." Lisa patted the old bike affectionately. She pulled two muddy leaves out of the front spokes.

Laurie was looking around as if she didn't want Lisa to be seen near anything as uncool as a bike rack. She grabbed Lisa's arm and pulled her toward the flagpole. "I'll give you a ride to school anytime in my Mustang."

"That's okay. I like riding."

Laurie shrugged and played with her one long earring. "Anyway, I wanted to tell you about homecoming. . . ."

Lisa interrupted instantly. "Good. I want to talk to you about homecoming, too."

"Great!" Laurie squealed. "I've been working hard on your campaign, you know, and everybody is just thrilled with the idea of you as princess. And wait until you hear who I got to escort you to the dance. You are going to just faint!"

No, thought Lisa. *Laurie, I'm afraid you're the one who may faint*. Lisa put her books down on the concrete retaining wall. She took a deep breath of the crisp fall air and looked Laurie straight in her big, heavily made-up eyes. "Laurie, I appreciate your nominating me and going to all this trouble, but I've decided not to run for homecoming princess."

There was a deadly silence. It was broken when a teacher stuck his head out of the main entrance and yelled at a stocky senior who was lighting up a cigarette. Laurie didn't even notice. She just stared at Lisa with a stunned look on her gorgeous face. "What?" she said breathlessly.

"I decided that I haven't been involved in enough activities at school to deserve it. I don't want to run, and I'm dropping out."

Laurie's face was beginning to turn ugly. Her full mouth was starting to curl. "You can't do that. You'd better not do that," Laurie threatened in a low, gruff voice.

Lisa was amazed at the transformation that was taking place before her very eyes. It was like the Incredible Hulk. No wonder Peter and his crowd disliked Laurie. As long as everything was going Laurie's way she was all cotton candy, but the minute people crossed her, they immediately discovered the razor blades underneath.

"I can't do it, Laurie."

"What is your problem, Lisa!" Laurie exploded. "I have done so much for you, and now you turn on me. I even asked John Marquette to take you to the dance. I mean, he's only an all-city wrestler and a football player and a fabulous hunk. What do you want from me? I cannot believe this." Laurie's hands were balled up in tight little fists.

Lisa had no problem staying calm. "I'm sorry that you worked so hard for me and now it won't count for anything. But that's the way I feel." Lisa kept her voice sweet and even. She knew that

Laurie would never admit the real reason why she was so upset.

"Well, what am I supposed to tell John? After what I had to go through to get him to take you."

Lisa couldn't help smiling at that little dig. Besides, she had once been in a class with John Marquette, and even though he was popular, he was far from her idea of the dream date.

"I can't believe you would do this to me."

Lisa looked down at her digital watch. First-period bell was in a few minutes. It was a good thing, because when Laurie heard what Lisa was going to say next, things could get very sticky.

"Laurie, I've found my own date for the dance. I am out of the princess contest, and that's the way it is."

Laurie stamped her foot, and one of her yellow boots sagged around her ankle. "Is it just that you don't want to go with Marquette? Is that it? I mean, if you have your own date, I don't care." Laurie pulled up her floppy boot. "Who are you going with?"

Lisa knew it was inevitable. Laurie would find out anyway. After holding back for a few seconds, Lisa let it out.

"Peter Lacey."

"Peter Lacey!" Laurie yelled immediately. The first period bell rang. It seemed to echo Laurie's cry, and suddenly Lisa felt a little sorry for her.

"Look, Laurie, I'm sorry to disappoint you. I have to go to class. See you later."

Lisa picked up her books and started walking toward the main entrance. When she looked back, she saw that Laurie was still standing near the flagpole, her arms angrily crossed over her chest. Lisa waved good-bye, but Laurie looked right through her, as though she were invisible.

Laurie rushed across the quad as soon as lunch period began and made straight for the radio station. The first four periods of the day had been devoted to figuring out a way to pay Peter and Lisa back. She was still so angry that she was actually mumbling under her breath as she walked.

"Lisa and Peter. Yuck. Peter Lacey and Lisa Chang. Oh, it makes me sick."

The grassy quad was damp from an overnight rain, and the earth was soft. Laurie dug her heels in with each furious step, leaving a trail of tiny dents behind her. When she got inside the building that housed the radio station, she forced herself to stop and calm down. What she had to do would take skill and control. She had to get hold of herself.

Laurie stood and breathed deeply. When she finally heard Peter's voice come over the hall loudspeaker, she redid her lipstick, combed her short hair, and continued toward the station.

Janie Barstow was standing in the small room that led to the control booth. With one long, skinny arm she was pulling records off the shelf one at a time. After checking each title, she bent down and entered the name in a large notebook.

Laurie approached slowly. Janie was so engrossed in her work that she didn't notice the intrusion until Laurie spoke.

"Hi, Janie," Laurie said sweetly.

Janie looked up, her long bangs half-covering her eyes. She smiled self-consciously. "Laurie, I didn't know you were on the air today," she said softly. Janie looked down at herself and tucked in a stray tail of her short-sleeved blouse.

"I'm not. I was just walking by, and I felt like talking. Do you mind?" Laurie peered inside the control room to make sure that Peter hadn't seen her. The door was closed, but Laurie could see through the window. Peter had his earphones on and his eyes closed. He was listening intently to the music.

"I don't mind," Janie answered shyly. She was obviously surprised that someone like Laurie would want to talk to her.

"Can we go out into the hall? Something's been bothering me that I want to get cleared up." Laurie leaned down to help Janie pick up a stack of records.

Janie put her pencil inside her notebook to hold her place. "Okay. Um, sure."

The two girls stepped into the hallway. Laurie closed the door leading into the station. "Janie, is it okay to close the door? Will Peter need you?"

Janie looked down at the gray floor. "I don't think so. He got all his records before he went on." There was a short silence. "But thanks."

"Sure. Well, this is very embarrassing but. . . ." Laurie paused and put her hand on Janie's arm. "I know I haven't been very nice to you sometimes, and I feel badly about it. I wanted you to know why so that you didn't think I was a totally awful person."

Janie looked up in amazement. "I never thought that," she insisted.

"This is hard to talk about, but —" Laurie looked away and made a dramatic pause — "it's just that I'm kind of jealous of you, Janie."

Janie's narrow mouth dropped open. Laurie Bennington, who had great looks, the best clothes, and was incredibly popular . . . Laurie Bennington, jealous of a washout like herself?

"Why would you be jealous of me?" Janie asked finally. She didn't have any idea of how to react.

Laurie sighed and managed to look sad. "You know that I used to like Peter, don't you?"

Janie was getting really confused. Why was Laurie telling her about Peter? "Yes, I heard something about that," Janie confessed softly.

"I guess I still do," Laurie admitted.

It certainly wasn't hard for Janie to understand how any girl could like Peter.

"Well, Janie. The one time I ever even got close to getting somewhere with him, he told me he wasn't interested because of his complicated feelings for you."

Janie's heart felt like it had just stopped. "He said that?"

"He talks about you a lot, and not just to me. He feels like you're the only person who really understands the radio station, and you know how important that is to him. He never thinks about anything else."

Janie was scared. It was as if Laurie had read her mind, her fantasies, and was now convincing her that her dreams could come true. Was Laurie trying to make her look like a fool?

And yet there was a core of truth to what Laurie was saying. Janie *was* the only girl who really cared about the station, and that *was* incredibly important to Peter.

"Peter and I are just friends," Janie whispered.

"I know. Peter is a little afraid that if it turned into something else it might ruin your working relationship. And with Peter, anything having to do with the radio station is top priority. That's why he's never made a move — yet. I'm just telling you what he told me."

Janie wanted to believe it. She knew that Peter was always more concerned with the station than he was with girls. But she also knew she wasn't pretty; she wasn't popular; she was too shy to talk half the time. Was it possible that Peter did actually like her? "I don't believe it," Janie said finally.

"Janie, he's been telling everybody how he can't wait for homecoming, how he's so excited about going with you. I'm telling you, it's the truth."

"But we're just doing the records together. It's not a date or anything."

"Have you ever known Peter to go on a real date? I'm telling you, this is the way he is about dating. I just wish it was me he was going with." Laurie looked away. "Don't tell anyone I said that, okay? Promise?"

"Okay."

"I can't believe you don't know he likes you.

It's so obvious to me. Like when I came in and you two were dancing together. No guy acts like that unless he's really stuck on a girl."

"You really think so?"

"I know so. Well, I've blabbed on enough. I don't know how I got into all this. All I wanted to do was make sure you understood why I've acted so strangely toward you. Oh — I wouldn't try to talk to Peter about it. Just get some great dress for homecoming and let it happen." Laurie patted Janie on the shoulder. "I'll see you next week for my show."

Janie watched Laurie's perfect figure as she turned the corner and disappeared. Her head was spinning. Could it be true? Janie had never known Peter to go on real dates. He had acted really excited when she offered to do the records with him. He'd been awfully nice to her, especially in the last few days. Maybe she wasn't as plain as she thought. Or maybe Peter didn't care about looks. After all, he had rejected Laurie. Maybe Peter saw the inner qualities that she knew she had but nobody else ever saw. Maybe he had somehow seen the real Janie Barstow.

Janie pulled open the door and slowly walked back into the station. Just when she arrived at the record shelf, Peter flung open the studio door and came running out. He gave her a wonderful smile and dropped his arm around her slim shoulder.

"Did you leave that carton of milk in the studio for me?" he asked with a playful glint in his eye.

Janie nodded. There was such a huge lump in her throat that she couldn't swallow.

"What would I do without you, Barstow? Huh? I'd be lost, totally lost!" With that, Peter gave her arm a squeeze before happily racing back to the control room.

Janie stood there paralyzed. If she had died right then, all she knew was that she would have died a very, very happy girl.

Chapter
16

The rain streamed down Lisa's face. Her hair was dripping, and her heavy cotton pants were soaked from the thighs down. They were a pair of new overdyed maroon jeans, and the color was running down her shins and staining the tops of her pink Nikes. Lisa barely noticed. All she could think about was how she had to see Peter. That was all that mattered.

Wiping the beads of water off the face of her watch, she saw that school had been out for twenty-five minutes. There was no way of knowing exactly where Peter was, but he couldn't go home without his Volkswagen. So that's where Lisa was waiting — right next to Peter's car, in the middle of the Kennedy parking lot. Lisa felt an icy splat of water hit the back of her neck and run down inside the collar of her wet nylon parka. She shivered, looked across the empty lot toward the football field, and continued to wait.

It was the first big rainstorm of the season, accompanied by lightning and roars of thunder. That was just how Lisa felt inside — turbulent and rumbling with doubt. She almost felt as if she were drowning; it was difficult to breathe and impossible to see clearly.

"LISA!"

At last she saw Peter coming toward her, his leather jacket pulled up over his head. He gave her a vigorous wave and began to run.

Lisa began to run, too. When she flew into Peter's arms, her wet face brushed his.

Peter let her go and looked at her. "Is anything wrong?" he asked quickly.

"I don't know."

Peter knit his brows together questioningly. He took her hand, and they rushed across the lot to his car. As quickly as he could, Peter fished out his keys and opened the door.

They climbed into the front, and Peter pulled the door closed with a hollow whack. The inside of the car was steamy and smelled of damp rubber. Peter reached behind the seat and removed a blue towel that was covering a collection of circuit boards. He handed the towel to Lisa.

"I thought you had to go to the physical therapist today," Peter said, taking the towel from Lisa when she was through and drying his own hair.

"I did. I ran here afterward to find you."

"Is your ankle going to be okay?"

"My ankle's fine." Lisa paused. She reached over and took Peter's hand in hers. She took a long look at his face, trying to memorize it. Green eyes, dark wavy hair, wide cheekbones. She would remember every detail.

"Peter."

"What?"

"Bielman called this afternoon."

"And . . ."

"He said yes."

"You mean . . ."

"He wants me to go to Colorado."

"He does?"

"He wants me to be there in a week."

"A week?"

"Yes."

Both their voices were dull and flat. For a few days, they had pretended there was no chance of this really happening. Now everything was changing. There was a long, painful pause.

Peter moved away sharply and avoided Lisa's eyes. It was as if something inside him had temporarily snapped. "So, that's great, right?" His voice was hard and angry.

"Yes. It is great." Lisa's tone was equally harsh.

"That's what you wanted. The Olympics and all that." His words still had a sharp edge.

"Yeah, it is what I wanted," Lisa insisted hotly. She had never felt Peter's anger before, and it put her on the verge of tears. "Why do you sound so mean?" she blurted out. "This is great news. We're supposed to be laughing and celebrating!" Lisa's voice was anything but happy.

"Why do you sound so mad?" Peter yelled

angrily. "Go out and celebrate if you want to. Laugh it up!"

Lisa raised her voice to match Peter's. "Well, I don't feel like going out and celebrating! This is the best day of my life, and I feel awful. And it's all your fault!"

"My fault! Why? Because you just spring this on me and I'm not jumping for joy?"

"No, stupid," Lisa shouted at the top of her lungs, "because I love you!"

Silence. The rain pounded on the roof of the car. A blurry flood was running down the windshield. Peter sunk down in his seat. Slowly he leaned over and rested his head on Lisa's shoulder.

"I love you, too," he said very softly. "Wouldn't you know, I finally really fall for a girl, and she goes off and leaves me."

"I know how you feel."

Lisa shifted to face Peter. He took her hands. They both let out a huge sigh at exactly the same time.

"Lisa," Peter reached up and pushed a wet strand of hair away from her cheek. "It was dumb to get mad, I know. It's great that Bielman wants you to go to Colorado. It's the best thing that could have happened."

"I know. Part of me is excited that he took me. Part of me is scared that I'll get there and everybody else will be better than I am. And part of me really hurts when I think about how we're just getting started and I have to go away."

Peter pulled her into his arms and kissed her.

Lisa tried to be aware of every sensation — the way he smelled, the softness of his mouth, the strong pressure of his arm around her back. She ran her hand along the sleeve of his heavy wool sweater — it was still damp around the neckline. Lisa would have to remember all of that, too.

"Hey, you steamed up the window." Peter cracked a smile.

Lisa looked up and saw that the windshield was foggy. She laughed softly and gave him a short punch in the ribs.

"I've decided there's only one thing to do," Peter said as he leaned forward.

"What's that?"

"Make the most of the time we have left. I mean, we are going to homecoming in a few days. So I say we make it the best night there ever was. Sound okay to you?"

Lisa nodded and smiled. She knew Peter was right. They would just have to make homecoming a night they would never forget.

"Brenda, at least think about it," Chris insisted. She edged back against the headboard of her bed and got up on her knees. Holding a small section of her stepsister's fine dark hair, she began to braid the strands. She felt Brenda pull away. "Don't move. I can't get all the layered parts when you do that."

Brenda sat still. She wore a dark blue nightshirt, and her angular cheeks were still pink from the shower. "Why would I want to go to the homecoming dance at all? All those snobby kids in their corny dresses. What a drag."

152

Chris remained patient. "I'm just saying that if you start doing things like going to the dance, kids will get to know you better. What's wrong with that?"

"They know plenty about me already, thanks to Laurie Bennington." Brenda held up a small hand mirror and looked at her head from different angles. Chris was attempting to cornrow her hair. "I look like a minus ten."

Chris paused a minute to rest her long, slender hands. She noticed that Brenda had pierced three holes in her left earlobe and was wearing tiny stud earrings. Chris almost asked her sister when and why she had done that, but she knew it was just another way for Brenda to show that she was different. Ever since Laurie had begun her destructive gossip campaign, Brenda had been acting more and more insecure. And even though Laurie had let up a little since Chris's radio interview, the damage had already been done. Chris picked up the comb again.

"Look, Woody Webster doesn't have a date, and he said he'd love to take you. He's a really nice guy."

Brenda whipped around, almost hitting Chris in the face with her wet hair. "Forget it, Chris! I don't want to go anywhere with some guy that you dug up. Why do you do stuff like that? Don't you think I could find my own date if I wanted one? Which, by the way, I don't!"

Chris knew that she had pushed Brenda too far. In the last month things between the two sisters had improved, and Chris didn't want to

153

jeopardize that. "All right. I'm sorry." Chris held up her hands.

Brenda sighed, stood up, and began to undo Chris's plaiting. "I know you're trying to help me. but please — don't defend me on the radio, don't fix me up on dates, just let me live my life my own way. Okay?"

"Okay," Chris answered flatly. She tapped the wet comb against her palm, sitting cross-legged on her bed.

Brenda moved toward the bedroom door. "Thanks for trying to do my hair. I'm going to go look at that history junk again."

Brenda turned, opened the door, and marched down the hall toward her own room.

Chris threw the comb against the wall. It bounced off and landed on the opposite twin bed, leaving a tiny mark on the pale blue wallpaper. How could she help someone who was as stubborn as Brenda? Sometimes it didn't even seem worth trying.

On the nightstand next to Chris's bed, the phone rang. Chris picked it up as her stepmother, Catherine, was saying hello.

"Hello, is Chris there?" the voice on the other end asked.

Chris immediately recognized Phoebe. There was an urgency in her best friend's tone.

"Catherine, I've got it up here."

"All right, dear." Catherine hung up the downstairs extension.

"Hi, Pheeb."

"Hi. I looked for you at school today."

"I had a chem makeup during lunch, and then

after school the rain was so bad I got a ride home with Woody's mom."

"Yeah. I got soaked."

Chris could tell there was a funny hesitation in Phoebe's voice, as if she had something on her mind that she couldn't quite bring herself to say.

Phoebe cleared her throat. "Did you pick up your homecoming dress?"

"Tomorrow. I can't wait." Chris had found a fabulous blue satin dress on sale at Saks. The store was repairing the slightly torn hem.

"Well, Chris," Phoebe said nervously, "since homecoming is so soon, I really have to know what you decided about my going to see Griffin. Can I tell my folks that I'm going to your house on Saturday night? That's all you have to do; just cover for me."

Chris felt like she was sinking. She knew she couldn't lie, and that even if she could there was a good chance that Phoebe wouldn't get away with it. She had been hoping that Phoebe would realize that it just wasn't possible for her to go to New York, no matter how much she wanted it. In her kindest voice, Chris explained her decision. "I understand how much you want to see Griffin. I'm sorry. I just don't think it would be right for me to lie for you."

"I understand. No, honest, Chris, I do. Thanks anyway."

"Phoebe, what are you going to do?"

"I don't know, Chris. I really don't know."

By the time Phoebe hung up the phone she

had thought about it long enough. She didn't blame Chris. She knew that lying wasn't the way Chris handled things. She also knew that if her parents found out, both of them would be in trouble.

Still, for Phoebe those concerns were minor compared with a chance to be with Griffin. If Chris wouldn't lie for her, someone else might. If she couldn't find a friend to cover for her, she would think of another plan. She didn't know what it would be, but she had to go to New York to see Griffin. She missed him way too much to wait any longer.

Chapter
17

Things were going right for Laurie Bennington.

First that substitute in French had believed her story about having to get out of class to do something for student council. Second, the hall monitor hadn't noticed her sneaking around the boys' gym looking for Peter. Next, some decent-looking junior had nearly dropped a barbell on himself when he saw her standing in the gym doorway. With no thought to his own risk, the boy had sneaked over at Laurie's beckoning, to let her know where she could find Peter.

Now Laurie peered down from the narrow hallway that spanned the area above Kennedy's two new handball courts. It was a boys-only day at the courts, but so far no one had seen her, and Laurie had the feeling that she was home free.

She breathed in the stuffy, humid air and hoped that it wasn't making her short hairdo lie too flat against her head. As she walked toward the second court, she turned up the collar of her wool jacket and fluffed her hair with her finger-tips. She wanted to look terrific when she found Peter and delivered her message. She wanted him to really suffer.

The coast was still clear. Laurie approached the court and looked down. Sure enough, Peter was playing. With delight Laurie saw that Peter was playing her homecoming date, Brad David-son.

They were both good athletes. Although Brad was taller and longer-limbed, Peter was a touch faster, and Laurie couldn't help noticing his muscular arms and the power with which he slapped the ball. There was no doubt that they were both attractive. Brad, so slim and clean-cut; Peter, strong and quick. Both with their shirts off, both with a single leather glove for serving, both breathing rapidly and wiping their brows.

They were playing hard. Their concentration was so intense that Laurie would have to make a point of attracting their attention. For a moment she let herself fantasize that the heat of the game was due to her. They were fighting over her. Oh, how she would love that. The echo and pop of the ball brought Laurie back to reality. Fantasies were fine, but right now she had something very real to accomplish.

Brad managed to return one of Peter's harder shots. Peter raced across the floor to reach it, finally diving and tipping the ball with the end of his fingers. The ball dribbled toward the wall,

158

and Peter sprawled onto the hardwood floor.

"Oh, man," Peter complained. He rubbed his palm and sat up. Brad extended an arm to help Peter stand. Both boys looked exhausted.

Laurie put her hands together. Her clapping echoed across the court. Brad and Peter looked up, but Peter was the first to speak.

"Hey, Bennington, who let you in here?" Brad quickly fetched his T-shirt and pulled it on. Peter picked his up, too, but only used it to wipe his face.

"It is public property, isn't it? I was just passing by and I wanted to watch you play." Laurie leaned fetchingly on the railing.

Peter gave Brad a disgusted look.

"Hi, Brad," Laurie said seductively. "We're going to have a great time at homecoming tonight."

Brad looked away. He didn't say anything.

"Oh, what about you, Peter? I guess you finally got a date for homecoming, didn't you?"

Peter started to pace like a lion in a cage. Laurie was glad that there was distance between them. Especially when he heard what she was going to say.

"Laurie, just leave Lisa alone, okay? She's out of the homecoming race, so just stay off her case."

"Lisa?" Laurie said in her most innocent voice. "Who said anything about Lisa? I mean, Lisa's not your date tonight. At least not from what I've heard." Laurie paused to smile at Brad. He was leaning in the corner of the court with his hands on his waist.

Peter threw the ball against the front wall. "Laurie, I don't know what you're talking about. Aren't you supposed to be in class or something? Come on, don't we get any peace in this school?"

"Peter," Laurie insisted, "I'm just confused. You know, all I've heard for the last few days is how Janie Barstow is your date for the dance tonight."

Peter laughed. "Janie? That's really out there. Who told you that? You've got your facts wrong, Bennington."

Peter shook his head and threw his T-shirt over his shoulder. "Let's go, Brad." Both boys started to walk toward the small door.

"Is that so, Peter? Funny, since I got the information right from Janie," Laurie said harshly.

Peter waved her off. "Janie is helping with the records between sets. She didn't mean we have a date."

"Really? Is that why she went out and bought an expensive dress? Is that why she's so excited she can barely stand it? Is all that because she's planning to sit in some dirty little equipment room and play the records?"

Peter stopped and turned around. Laurie smiled slightly and kept going.

"Janie told me flat out that you asked her to go to homecoming with you and she accepted. I've been in the studio with her when you talked about it. Even I thought you'd asked her from the way you acted. Come on, Peter. You must have noticed how Janie melts every time you look at her. How insensitive are you? You lead poor Janie on and then ask somebody else?"

Peter put a hand to his forehead. There was a worried look in his eyes. Laurie leaned over further to see if Brad was still in the doorway. "It's a good thing girls like Janie have girls like me to look out for them. Bye, Brad. Seven-thirty, right? Mmmm. See you then."

With a feeling of real triumph, Laurie swung the long strap of her shoulder bag over her arm and trotted back down the hall. This time she was spotted by Coach Cohen, the tall, gawky baseball coach. He looked at her questioningly, but she held herself with such confidence that he didn't even think of stopping her.

Peter entered the locker room and hurried into the shower. He turned the water on as hard as it would go and let it beat on his back. He hoped it wasn't true. Laurie was just trying to get to him again. Maybe it was all a joke. Janie was his friend, his co-worker. He had never been inter-ested in her in any other way, and surely Janie knew it. Of course Janie knew it.

Peter thought of asking Brad for advice. But his friend seemed as troubled as he was — those dark moods he'd been having ever since Phoebe had broken up with him. Perhaps just thinking about his evening ahead with Laurie had made Brad feel even worse.

Peter yelled good-bye to Brad and bolted out of the locker room and across the quad. It was windy and cool, and with each gust the trees were stripped of a few more leaves. Peter could feel the goose bumps up and down his arms.

"Janie can't really think that!"

He tried to remember back to what he could have said to make Janie assume he had asked her to the dance. They had talked about doing the records, but it was never a formal date. Or was it? Starting to feel sick, Peter realized that he had never told Janie about Lisa. Things with Lisa had happened so quickly, and he saw Janie only when he did his radio show.

Quickly he headed down the hall to the station. When he looked in, he felt his stomach do a nervous somersault. Janie was already there. Her jacket was hanging on the hook near the shelves, and he could hear her bustling around inside the studio.

Peter approached the control booth.

"Hi, Janie."

Janie looked up, her face expectant and pale. "You weren't supposed to see me. It was a surprise."

Janie moved aside and Peter saw a plate of homemade cookies sitting on the control board. "For me?" Peter choked out.

Janie nodded and smiled shyly. "I made them."

Peter nervously tasted a cookie. It was a Tollhouse chocolate chip. Normally that was Peter's favorite. This time it caught in his throat.

"Good. Thanks, Janie."

"I was going to make peanut butter, but then I remembered the last time I made chocolate chip and. . . ." Janie brushed the hair away from her eyes. "Um, Peter, I wanted to ask you. Um . . . do you like yellow?"

"Yellow?" There was a long pause. "Why?"

Janie looked down. "Well, I got a new dress for tonight, and it's yellow."

"Oh."

"You don't like it? I had a really hard time choosing. There were so many different. . . ."

Peter cut in. "Janie, I want to make sure we have our signals straight. About the dance tonight. . . ."

"Oh, yeah. I guess we should get there kind of early, huh?" Janie said softly.

"What?" She had totally missed his meaning.

"For the records."

"Oh. Right."

"Um, so, what time do you want me to be ready by? I don't mind if we have to get there real early. Anything for the radio station. You know that."

Janie's eyes were two pools of total sweetness. Peter just couldn't believe how innocent she was, and how stupid he'd been. He wasn't looking at the eyes of a pal, someone who just happened to care about the radio station as much as he did. They were the eyes of a girl lost in a complete and overwhelming crush. He'd really taken Janie for granted. How could he have been so insensitive? Peter wanted to sink to his knees and crawl under the control board.

And there was something else in Janie's brown eyes. It looked almost like fear. She was pleading with him not to burst her bubble, not to destroy the hopes she wasn't quite sure she should have.

Janie looked down at her watch. "Peter, aren't you going to start your show?"

"Oh, right," Peter exclaimed. He began flicking switches and turning dials. Looking up at the wall clock he saw he was a minute late. In a dash he threw a record on the turntable and climbed into his chair. He turned on the mike and cued the music.

"Hey, there, Cardinals, this is WKND." He knew his voice sounded forced and strained, but he kept going. "Bet you thought we'd never get on the air. Well, fooled ya. Got a great pre-homecoming program of rock 'n' roll coming up, so let's get down and get with it!"

Peter hit the button for the music, switched off the microphone, and sighed. Homecoming might be his last chance to really be with Lisa. They didn't have much time left together.

Janie was standing in the doorway looking worried. She stared down at her feet and slowly moved a ball of dust along the floor. Peter felt a thousand needles in his heart. What was he supposed to do? How had he gotten himself into this mess?

For a second it looked like Janie knew exactly what he was thinking. Her face turned white, and a glazed, painful look came into her eyes. She started to turn and walk out of the booth.

Peter stopped her.

"Janie?"

"Yes?"

"I'll pick you up at seven."

Chapter
18

The wind was loud and gusty, but Lisa could still hear Peter's voice coming over the speakers in the quad. Each song he played seemed to be tailored just for them, whether it was a love song, a sad song, even the boisterous rock 'n' roll. Each one reflected just the way she felt inside — excited, expectant, sad, scared, confused, alive.

"So, who will you live with in Colorado?" Chris Austin asked, her blue eyes wide and curious. She was leaning against an old tree and had Ted's letterman's jacket slung over her shoulders.

"At first I'll live with this divorced woman and her two daughters. We'll see if that works out. She sounded really nice on the phone." Lisa sat cross-legged on a bench in the crowd's famous lunchtime spot. It was her first time at this daily gathering place. Yet as she looked at the warm faces around her, she felt like anything but a stranger.

"I think it sounds really exciting," bubbled Sasha Jenkins. "Maybe you'll live in a solar house. People in Colorado are really into that." Sasha pulled the cuffs of her heavy South American sweater over her hands and cocked her head to one side.

"Maybe we could all do a ski trip or something like that and come visit you," Phoebe added. It was the first thing she'd said all through lunch. Lisa sensed that her normally bubbly and cheerful friend was preoccupied today.

"You paying? I'll go," Woody joked

"Lisa, it's great that you're going to homecoming," Ted added. He was sitting on the ground next to Chris. He gave Lisa a special smile. Lisa figured it was a thank-you for dropping out of the princess race.

"Oh, guess what!" Sasha said to Lisa. "Yesterday Woody and I decided since neither of us had a date that we'd go together. So we'll be there, too. I still don't have anything to wear."

"You'd better find something quick. I refuse to escort a naked woman to homecoming," Woody cracked. "It would look bad on my transcript."

Ted laughed. "Hey, I like the idea; maybe we could get all the girls to do that." Chris slapped him on the top of his head.

The laughter died down and Sasha and Chris began to discuss Sasha's homecoming article for the newspaper. Ted and Woody started going over the football game to be played on Saturday night, while Phoebe listened quietly.

Lisa looked at her friends and wondered how

166

she had managed to exist without them. In the future, whether she was in Colorado or busy with the heaviest training schedule, she had to make the effort to keep these people in her life. Just being in their comfortable circle made her feel relaxed and whole. It was a very different circle than the one she used to think about, the one that isolated her from the rest of the world. This was a wide, expansive circle that had lots and lots of room in it.

Lisa smiled to herself and leaned over her legs to stretch her calves. She felt a slight tug in her ankle and for the first time felt grateful for her troublesome old injury. Had it not been for her bad ankle, she would never have been given this week to rediscover her friends. Or to go to homecoming.

"Do you think my article should be about all the homecoming winners?" Sasha was asking.

Lisa started to answer but noticed that Phoebe had moved even further away from the others. She was staring off toward the student council room and chewing nervously on the end of a plastic spoon. Lisa remembered that Phoebe wasn't going to homecoming.

"Phoebe, are you okay?" Lisa asked. "I guess it's pretty boring to hear us go on and on about homecoming."

Phoebe gave a sad smile. Her red hair was tied back, but a few stray curls framed her face. "Oh no, go ahead. I don't mind." Phoebe looked off again. Her green eyes were filled with worry. Whatever was bothering her, she seemed to want to keep it to herself.

167

There was a long silence, broken by Peter's voice coming out of the loudspeakers as he signed off the air. Lisa looked at her watch. Strange. Lunch was only half over. Knowing how Peter loved his radio time, Lisa wondered why he would stop his show early.

"I'm telling you, just don't be afraid to throw the long bomb and you guys will have it made," Lisa heard Woody say loudly.

"Yeah, if I can count on my front line," Ted answered. Then he turned to Lisa and pointed across the quad. "Hey Lisa, I think Peter wants you."

Lisa looked up and saw Peter standing near the building that housed the radio station. He had one hand in the pocket of his baggy army-surplus pants and was gesturing at her with the other. Lisa immediately ran over to meet him.

"Hi," he said dully as she came up next to him. He didn't reach out to hug her or even take her hand. It was obvious something was very wrong. With a flick of his head he gestured for her to follow him back inside the building and down a side hallway. Finally, he stopped in a quiet corner and leaned against the wall. "What a mess," he exhaled.

"What?"

"Tonight."

"What about tonight?"

"The dance. I think we have a big problem. Or rather, I have a big problem, and since you're my date you do, too. I'm sorry. Man, what a huge drag."

Lisa tried to figure out what Peter meant as he

168

nervously slapped his hands together. Had his car broken down, had someone in his family gotten sick, had the gym been blown up? What was it?

"Lisa," Peter said in a flat voice, "I'm not sure how to explain this but . . . I think I have another date."

This was the last thing Lisa had expected to hear. She trembled slightly.

"What? I don't get it." She heard the edge in her voice.

"That makes two of us." Peter looked off and blinked hard. "You know Janie Barstow, my assistant at the station?"

"Of course."

"You know what she's like. Nice, but really vulnerable. Anyway, I had mentioned to her that she could do the records with me, and I went in today and it's obvious that she thinks we have a date. She bought a new dress and she's all excited. . . ." Peter cleared his throat. "Lisa, what am I supposed to do? You should have seen the look in her eyes. I don't know how this happened."

Lisa felt all the excitement rush out of her body. She was limp. It was as if someone had given her the most wonderful present and then turned around and taken it right back.

"It's my own dumb fault," Peter said. "I should have seen it. I should have picked up that she had a crush on me. I guess I got so involved in the radio, and you, that I missed this stuff that's right under my nose. How could I be so dumb?"

Lisa leaned against the opposite wall and looked at Peter. Neither of them said anything.

It was a no-win situation. From just the few times they'd met, Lisa knew how fragile Janie's ego was, how hurt she would be by any rejection. Peter's standing her up would make Janie never want to show her face at Kennedy again.

"I think you should take her," Lisa heard herself saying. This time her voice wasn't edgy or hard. She had learned a lot about giving and sharing lately. Maybe this was just one more lesson.

"What?" Peter's eyes were filled with confusion.

"I think you'd better take Janie."

"Oh, Lisa, this was our night," he shook his head. "But what else am I going to do?"

They were both silent again. Lisa felt a sudden pressure in the back of her throat and knew she was about to cry. As she thought about what it would mean for her to stay home, the tears began to run down her cheeks in a steady stream.

"This doesn't mean I want you to change your mind," Lisa managed through her tears. "I'm just upset, but" — she sniffed loudly — "taking Janie's the right thing to do."

Peter took a step forward, put his arms around her, and held her very tightly. It was almost like they were starting to say good-bye, a practice for the farewell that would come much too soon.

Lisa lifted her face and looked into Peter's troubled eyes. She stood up on her tiptoes and began to kiss him. As soon as she met his lips he pulled her in even closer.

Just then they both heard a soft gasp and instinctively broke apart. They turned and saw her at the same time. Janie Barstow was standing no more than three feet away from them.

Janie's face was drained of all color and her eyes were filled with pain. Just looking at her made Lisa ache. Janie turned around and started to run away.

"Janie, wait!" Peter took two quick steps and grabbed her slender wrist. Janie hid her face, but it was obvious that she was crying.

"Janie, we have to talk," Peter said in his kindest voice. But before he even managed to finish his sentence, Janie let out a loud sob. It was as if something had burst within her. She was shaking. Lisa stepped back while Peter moved in and touched Janie's arm.

"I was just . . . the play list . . . for the dance," Janie wept incoherently. She held a crumpled piece of paper in her hand. It was the list of records for the homecoming dance. Peter gently took it from her. Her body shook harder and her sobs grew more violent.

"You never wanted to go with me to the dance, did you?" Janie cried. She was like a fragile tree being tossed around in a wild storm. Peter stepped in to hug her.

"I'm so stupid," Janie moaned. "I'm such a fool."

"No, you're not," Peter soothed.

"Yes, I am." Janie paused, trying to catch her breath. "I should have known you would never like someone like me."

"I do like you, Janie. You're one of my most important friends. This is just an awful misunderstanding," Peter tried to explain.

"I should never have listened to Laurie!" Janie

171

cried. "She was being so nice to me, and I guess I wanted to believe her. Oh, I'm such a jerk."

"Laurie?" Peter stepped back and made Janie look at him. "You mean, Laurie told you. . . ."

"I didn't believe her at first. She said you told her you really liked me and that I was your date for homecoming." Janie's voice was more level. "But then you acted so . . . I don't know, happy to see me and. . . ." Janie shuddered and started to cry again.

Peter's face was turning red with rage. "I don't believe she would do this. Even Laurie Bennington. I never thought she was *this* low."

Lisa stepped back over and handed Janie a Kleenex. Janie's whole face was swollen and pink.

"Janie, I think you should just go with Peter and have a great time and look Laurie straight in the eye. Show her she can't play with you like that," Lisa urged.

Janie's crying began to build again. "Oh no, I can't do that. Just forget about me. I'm sorry. I don't want to ruin your homecoming."

Suddenly Peter stood up very straight. His eyes were decisive and clear. It was the first time he had looked like himself that afternoon.

"I think I know what to do."

Lisa looked at him. Janie stopped crying and gave him her attention, too. There was something about the urgency in his voice that gave them both hope.

Peter began looking around madly, snapping his fingers with renewed energy. "Janie, will you go to the dance tonight if I promise you that

172

you'll be able to look Bennington in the face and smile? Will you do that? Promise me you'll still go to the dance."

"You can trust Peter. You know that," Lisa urged.

"What about you?" Janie said to Lisa in a tiny voice. Lisa looked up at Peter as if to ask the same question.

Peter interrupted. "Don't worry. If I can make this work out we'll all be okay. Lisa, will you get ready to go tonight, too?"

"You mean to the dance?"

"Yes."

"But Peter. . . ." Both girls looked skeptical.

"Believe me, I think we can work this out. Just trust me, okay?"

Janie looked at Lisa and Lisa looked at Janie.

"So both of you be ready. Promise."

Both girls managed to smile at each other. "Okay," Lisa said, "I'll be ready."

Janie shrugged her thin shoulders and wiped her nose. "Okay," she whispered. "I'll go."

Peter met Lisa's eye and smiled. Lisa had no idea what he had in mind. She just prayed with all her heart that it would work.

Chapter
19

"Try this color on your eyelid."

"Like this?"

"That looks good."

"Lisa, are you sure?"

Lisa nodded and tried to ease Janie's apprehension. Poor Janie was still shaky and scared and full of doubts about the evening ahead. It was almost seven. Peter was supposed to arrive any minute.

Lisa was glad that she had talked Janie into coming over and getting ready at her house. Lisa's parents were out visiting her older brother in Washington, D.C., and Lisa was having her own share of nerves about the evening ahead. She needed company as much as Janie did.

Janie stood up and began to pace back and forth across Lisa's bedroom. She wore low beige heels that tapped nervously against the hardwood floor. Lisa collapsed on her bed and brushed her hair for the fifth time.

"Who's that?" Janie asked shyly, pointing to a framed photograph on Lisa's wall. She tugged on her bangs and gave an anxious look at the alarm clock on Lisa's desk.

"That's John Curry. He's my favorite skater," Lisa answered. She knew Janie was just trying to keep her mind off the present situation. There was a long silence.

Lisa couldn't sit still either. She walked over to the window seat and parted the short, pleated curtains. No sign of Peter yet. He had called Lisa earlier and filled her in on the details of his plan. But he had no idea whether or not his scheme would work. Lisa would find out when he arrived — very shortly.

"Oh, I'm sorry," Janie gasped as she nervously dropped the plastic pot of eyeshadow. It rolled toward the closet, making a hollow sound.

Lisa quickly scooped it up. "Don't worry." She patted Janie on the shoulder and took a deep breath.

Janie nodded and began to play with a loose thread on her dress. She was wearing an old-fashioned-looking yellow cotton outfit with bits of lacy trim. The dress had a drop waist and slightly gathered skirt that hung to the middle of Janie's calves. When Janie held her head up, she actually looked quite lovely. There was an understated beauty in her face that was complemented by her simple dress.

"Oh," Janie remembered suddenly, "I brought

this for you. I didn't know what color your dress was, but I think it goes." She pulled a small paper bag out of her purse and handed it to Lisa.

Lisa unwrapped a delicate green-blue flower made of stiff cloth. It was almost the same blue as her silk dress, and Lisa felt her eyes dampen as she got up to pin it into her hair.

"Janie, it's beautiful. Thanks." Lisa looked in the mirror. Her hair was falling in an even curve; her make-up was light but carefully applied; she had on her brand-new dress with the floppy collar and wide sash belt. She almost started to laugh. Here she was all dressed up, and there was a chance that she wasn't going anywhere.

"What are you laughing at?" Janie asked.

"Nothing. Just nerves, I guess." Lisa smiled and fastened the flower just above her ear. The brilliant blue made her eyes look even darker and more exotic. "Janie, thank you so much."

Janie looked down at her feet and smiled very slightly. "Well, I wanted to let you know — I mean you didn't have to — oh, you know."

"I know." Lisa went over and patted Janie's hand. "Stand up. Let's see how you look."

Janie stood up, her elbows pressed to her sides, her hands gripped together. Lisa had talked her into pinning back the sides of her hair so the cheekbones of her sweet, angular face were exposed. But even Lisa's gaze made Janie self-conscious and she turned away. She didn't like being looked at.

"Janie, you look great."

Janie was embarrassed. "I do?"

"Cross my heart."

The girls waited nervously for a few more minutes. Lisa checked the window again. Still no Peter.

"Janie, let's go down to the den. Okay?"

Janie nodded and followed Lisa down the stairs and into the large family room. The girls sat stiffly on the floral couch, each with a coat and purse in her lap.

When the doorbell finally rang, Lisa leapt up. She and Janie looked at each other. At the same time, they rushed to the front door. As they approached, Lisa tried to see through the panels of amber glass that were on either side of the entrance. It was impossible to make anything out. Lisa opened the door.

"Hi," said Peter.

He was wearing the oddest combination of clothes: old tuxedo jacket, bow tie, jeans, and high-top tennis shoes. It reminded Lisa of her own half-and-half way of dressing and she thought he looked wonderful. But Peter's clothes were not what mattered. What was really important was who was standing next to him. It was Brad Davidson.

Janie looked confused and still a little frightened. She backed up as Brad and Peter came into the entry hall.

"Janie," Peter said slowly, "do you know Brad Davidson?"

Janie held out a timid hand for Brad to shake.

Peter continued. "Janie, the four of us will go together, okay? A double date. Is that all right with you?"

Janie looked back and forth from Peter to

Lisa. Finally she shifted her gaze to Brad. "But what about Laurie? I thought you were taking Laurie Bennington."

Brad held his arm out to Janie and smiled broadly. "A guy's allowed to change his mind, isn't he?"

Janie paused and looked back at Lisa. Lisa gave her new friend a smile and a nod. Shyly, Janie took Brad's arm.

Lisa squeezed Peter's hand and the four of them walked out into the perfectly clear fall evening.

Laurie Bennington was starting to panic. The collar of her red gabardine jacket was feeling a little too high around her neck. The cuffs of her white crepe blouse were too tight around her wrists. Her palms were damp and her stomach was knotted. Brad was a half hour late. Something was very wrong.

She hadn't finished getting ready until after Brad was scheduled to arrive because she figured a boy should always wait. It helped to build his anticipation. She had wanted to make an entrance and watch Brad's eyes light up as he saw her walk into the living room in her wide-shouldered jacket and short straight skirt. He would have noticed the way her high heels and short hem showed off her legs, the way the deep red jacket offset her clear, olive skin. But by eight o'clock Laurie had been unable to stay in her room any longer. She wanted Brad to arrive, and she didn't want to wait a second longer.

She checked herself in the hall mirror and went

over to the front door. She had controlled herself until now, not looked outside. What if Brad was walking up just as she was anxiously peering out. That was not Laurie's style. Still, at this point Laurie didn't know what else to do. She opened the door and looked out into the quiet, empty street.

As she pushed the door open, she heard an odd sound. It was a rustling, a sliding, like a few leaves falling to the ground. She had just decided to ignore the sound when she saw the gleaming white envelope that had dropped on the edge of the doormat. It had Laurie's name on it.

She stepped back inside and read the note.

> Dear Laurie,
>   I thought it was great that you took the time to tell Peter about his date with Janie —you know, at the handball courts. Seeing how concerned you were for Janie, I knew you would understand when I told you that I had the same problem (as Peter, that is). Yes, I also have another date. And you convinced me that the decent thing to do is to honor it. Sorry to break *our* date at the last minute, but you know how things are.
>   Brad.

Laurie was steaming. She wanted to yell, to kick, to tear Brad apart with her bare hands. How dare he do this to her? To Laurie Bennington? HOW DARE HE!

Her hands were clenched so tightly her knuckles were turning white and her nails were digging into her palms. What was she going to do? She had to go to homecoming. As social activities officer it was her job to open the envelope and announce the winner for junior homecoming princess. She had to be there!!

Laurie swooped down the hall and grabbed her small beaded handbag. She would just drive herself. She would get in her Mustang and drive over to school. On the way she would figure out exactly how to handle Brad Davidson.

With a fierce slam of the front door, Laurie ran across the yard and climbed into her white Mustang. She gunned the motor so hard that a huge cloud of exhaust billowed behind her as she pulled away from the curb.

When she sped through an amber light at the corner of Rose Hill and Orange, it all came to her. Of course. Why hadn't she thought of it before? Phoebe Hall. That was why Brad had stood her up. Phoebe had changed her mind and snapped her fingers and Brad had come running back. There they would be at the dance, their arms around each other, all lovey-dovey — like nothing had ever happened.

Well, Laurie would fix that. She knew all about that flakey Griffin who had run off to New York. And she would make sure to remind Brad about him. She wouldn't let Brad forget a thing.

Laurie sped into the Kennedy parking lot, her brakes screeching as she pulled into one of the few spaces still left. Everybody was there already. She could see the lights coming from the gym, on the other side of the parking lot.

The music grew louder as Laurie approached.

She recognized Peter's favorite Bruce Springsteen album. Peter! At least she had succeeded there. His homecoming couldn't be going much better than hers.

Laurie stood in the doorway to the gym, her face in the shadows. The last thing she wanted was for other kids to know she had been stood up. If she just lay low until she had to make the princess announcement and then disappeared, perhaps nobody would suspect that things had gone so wrong for her. As she slipped into the gym and sneaked toward a remote corner, her eyes searched the dance floor for Phoebe's red hair. That was her first priority. Revenge.

The dance was in full swing. Most of the kids were dancing, trying to communicate with their dates above the blasting music or attacking the punch and cookie table. The Movers and Shakers, the band Laurie had hired from D.C., was busy getting ready for their next set. But Laurie ignored them, continuing to search for Phoebe and Brad. She thought she was getting close when she spotted Chris and Ted, dancing energetically. Laurie was surprised to see Chris in a low-cut satin dress. Her blonde hair was curled and bounced over her shoulders. Although Laurie had to admit that Chris looked great, she was convinced that she saw Brenda's trashy influence in the outfit.

Next to Chris and Ted were Woody and Sasha. Sasha was wearing a lacy antique dress and Woody was in red suspenders, of course, and a weird string tie. They were laughing and dancing a kind of jitterbug, with Woody trying to lift

181

Sasha over his head. Laurie decided they were ridiculous.

There was a loud cackle of feedback as the record ended and the band picked up their instruments. It was then that Laurie spotted Brad. He was walking out of the small equipment room on the side of the gym, where the sound system was housed. His jacket was slung over his arm, and he was smiling. Laurie stopped and waited for Phoebe.

But Phoebe wasn't behind him. Laurie watched with amazement as Lisa Chang followed Brad out of the equipment room. After Lisa came Janie Barstow. After Janie came Peter Lacey.

When the band blasted their first chord, Peter led Lisa out onto the dance floor. Their intimate smiles made Laurie tremble with anger. But what was even worse was when Brad took Janie Barstow's hand and escorted her onto the floor. Janie and Brad were smiling, too.

"I don't believe it," Laurie hissed to herself. "I just don't believe it!"

Could it be true? Had Brad actually decided to take Janie to the dance instead? How could anyone headed for the Ivy League be so vacant. Didn't Brad have eyes? Couldn't he see? Didn't he know that Janie was one of the most hopeless girls in the whole junior class?

Laurie shook her head.

"What's wrong, Laurie?" Annie Burke, a girl in her history class, was casting a mildly sympathetic look at her and extending her hand. "Are you feeling okay?"

"Okay? *I'm* fine!!" Laurie shouted. "It's every-

182

body else. . . ." Suddenly Laurie stopped. Her voice was too loud, and two couples had stopped dancing to stare at her. Annie had a funny expression on her face and had backed away.

"What I mean is," Laurie explained more calmly, "homecoming is always such a surprise."

Annie smiled. "Yes, I guess it is. I can't wait to find out who's princess!"

Laurie made herself smile back, but she knew in that instant she had been defeated. Peter had won. He had gotten his homecoming with Lisa, a homecoming for Janie, and humiliation for her.

This had to be the worst day of Laurie's life. And it wasn't over, either. As the band came to the end of their song, Brad made his way to the microphone, applause filling the large room. When it died down, Brad announced that it was time to find out who had won as the queen and her court.

There was no escape for Laurie. She climbed up onto the platform with dozens of eyes watching her every step. She sat in a folding chair facing the audience and waited while Liza Blume won for freshman princess and Alison Forbes took the sophomore crown. Laurie thought they were both boring and badly dressed. With a controlled walk, Laurie approached the microphone to announce her class's winner.

Laurie really looked into the audience for the first time. There they were, in the front on the right side, the whole group of them: Peter and Lisa, Brad, Janie, Sasha and Woody, Chris and Ted. The whole crowd except Phoebe.

Principal Beaman handed Laurie the envelope.

She opened it and wasn't surprised to see the name of the winner. Of course the crowd would go wild. Laurie gritted her teeth.

"Junior homecoming princess . . . Chris Austin." Laurie smiled tightly and watched Chris jump into Ted's arms while the whole group exploded.

"YAAAAAAY!" shouted Woody.

"You won!!!" screamed Sasha, hugging both Ted and Chris.

"All right!" yelled Peter.

As Chris ran up to the platform, her face flushed with joy, all Laurie could think of was that she was glad she had found out about the crowd before she'd wasted too much more time on them. They were a drag. Laurie hated them. And she was finally convinced that she wanted nothing whatsoever to do with any of them, ever again.

Chapter
20

The lights were dim and they cast long, elegant shadows across the ice. It was cold and drafty, but Peter and Lisa didn't feel it. Their arms were wrapped too tightly around each other.

"It's pretty amazing in here at night," Peter whispered, looking up at the vaulted, tin ceiling of the Capitol Ice Rink. The only sounds were the voices from the small television set in Mr. Helde's office and the constant hum of the cooling system.

Lisa sat next to Peter on the top bleacher and looked down at the empty oval of ice. When they had passed the rink after the dance, Peter had spotted the light in Mr. Helde's office, and they'd decided to go in. Lisa's old teacher hadn't minded taking a break from his late-night bookkeeping to answer the door. Lisa was leaving for Colorado the next morning, and he understood her sentimental reasons for wanting to be in that rink one last time.

Lisa snuggled in close to Peter and gave his bow tie a tug. He laughed softly and kissed her temple.

"What a crazy night," Lisa sighed. It was definitely one evening she would never forget.

"I think Janie ended up feeling okay, don't you?" Peter asked. He ran his hand along the back of Lisa's hair.

"I think so."

"She and Brad aren't destined to become the couple of the century, but I think they both had a pretty good time. It all worked out okay."

"I thought Laurie was going to choke when she had to announce Chris's name."

"Yeah. Me too." They both laughed. Peter slipped his arms under Lisa's. "So, how'd you like helping with the records? You think you might want to give all this up and become a DJ some day?" Peter gestured toward the ice with his head.

Lisa knew that they were trying to avoid the real subject. They had to figure out a way to say good-bye and they both knew it. She pushed back the wavy hair that was falling over Peter's forehead. Without saying anything, she rested her head on his shoulder and reached her arms up around his neck. Peter's hands slid down to the small of her back, and he held her with a strong grip. They stayed like that for a long time.

Finally Lisa turned to look back at the ice. "You know, I practically grew up in this rink.

I spent more time here than I ever did at school, maybe even more than at home."

Peter listened and kept his arms around her.

"It's strange to think of leaving it. It's like I'm leaving behind a huge part of my life. . . ."

"Because you're going ahead to live a new part."

"Yeah. I guess so. It's just that sometimes this place seemed like the whole world to me. I used to feel that this was the only place that really existed. And you know what?"

"What?"

"I think that's what was wrong. This isn't the whole world. It's important to me, and I want to skate as well as I can. But there are a lot of other things, too. Right?"

"Right."

"Like other people that you care about." There was a short silence.

"Yeah. It's pretty easy to get so involved in your own thing that you don't see the other stuff that's right under your nose. Like the whole mess with Janie."

Lisa touched the blue flower that was still pinned in her hair. "I'm kind of scared that when I get to Colorado it will be even worse."

"Why?"

"Oh, because I'll be with all the very best skaters, the ones who've really given up everything else just to skate. I've met lots of those kids at competitions before. They act as if they'll just die if they get a low score, or if they don't place. That's all they are, skaters, and if they aren't the

187

best then they think they're nothing. I don't want that to happen to me. I just want to remember that there's a world outside of the ice rink." Lisa knew she had finally broken out of that circle and she never wanted to get locked back in.

"Hey. I know." Peter cupped her face in his hands and kissed her gently on the mouth. "Every time you go into the skating rink in Colorado, the first thing you do. . . ." Peter smiled to himself.

"What?"

"Okay. The first thing you gotta think about is me." He gave a mischievous smile. "See, you think about me, and then you remember Rose Hill and all the rest of us here, and wonder how we are and what we're doing. So then, right away, you know there's a lot more than just that ice in Colorado."

Lisa started to laugh. Peter looked playful, too, but she knew that there was truth to what he was saying.

"And then. . . ." Peter's face suddenly became more serious.

"Yes."

"You remember that I love you and I'm thinking about you and I miss you . . ." Peter looked away, a little embarrassed, "and all that."

"I will, Peter. I will. I love you so much."

Lisa felt as if she might cry. But she didn't. Because she also felt so much joy that it balanced out the pain of leaving Peter. She knew that there would be so much of him — of all her friends — that she would take with her.

"Will you write?" Lisa whispered.

"Sure will. May even call. I'll send you wild cassette tapes. I guess you'll be too far away to get my show."

"I guess."

They smiled at each other. The television in Mr. Helde's office was silent. A moment later his light went out.

"You two still up there," the old man yelled. He was standing in the doorway of his office.

"We're coming," Lisa called back. She and Peter clutched each other's hands and climbed down to the bottom of the bleachers. "Thanks," Lisa said to her old teacher.

Mr. Helde patted Lisa's hand and looked over at Peter. "She's a good girl. I'll be sad to see her go. But it's for the best. I will miss her, but I'm happy that she will go."

"I think I know how you feel," Peter said, more to himself than anyone else.

"Ya." Helde pulled on his gray mustache, opened the front door, and said goodnight, giving Lisa a warm hug and shaking Peter's hand.

Lisa and Peter went out into the pitch black parking lot and walked over to Peter's car.

"You know something," Peter said as they slid into the front seat.

"Hmmm."

"Somehow I have the feeling that you haven't seen the last of me."

"Honest?"

"Don't worry," Peter teased as he started the engine, "if I can figure out a way to get a ticket to see Bruce Springsteen, I can certainly figure out a way to stay in touch with a girl I'm crazy about."

"You'd better." Lisa started to laugh and grabbed Peter in a fierce embrace.

Chapter
21

The dance had ended hours ago, but Phoebe had barely noticed. She barely noticed that her mother had brought her a piece of chocolate cake, or her father said goodnight. She had barely noticed anything but the telephone, and the terrible uneasiness she felt inside.

Griffin had said he would call on Thursday to plan their weekend meeting in New York. Phoebe had convinced Sasha to cover for her on Saturday night. But then the strangest thing had happened. Or, rather, hadn't happened. Griffin hadn't called. He had never forgotten to call before.

Phoebe had tried his number over and over, but there was never any answer. Every hour of the last day had been torture. Where was he and why hadn't he gotten in touch?

"Phoebe, sweetheart, I'm going to bed." Her mother paused in the doorway of the cluttered

191

living room. "Is there anything you want to talk about?"

Phoebe shook her head and stared at the television. It was some confusing movie about a girl diving for buried treasure.

"Go to sleep, Phoebe. Whatever it is, it will be better in the morning." Her mom came over, kissed her on the forehead, and left the room.

Better in the morning. Phoebe hoped so. If Griffin called, it would be better in the morning. If she knew what was going on and was sure that he was all right, it would be better in the morning. *Oh please, let him be all right! Please, please, let him call!* she pleaded silently.

Phoebe curled up in her father's rocker and hugged a pillow to her chest. The movie ended and another came on. Phoebe's eyes were starting to close. She was so tired. Her head became heavy and started to fall back against the wooden slats of the chair.

She bolted up when she heard the loud ring. Her heart was pounding and she almost tripped over her brother's jigsaw puzzle as she ran into the kitchen to answer the phone.

The first thing she heard when she picked it up was her father's groggy voice.

"Who? What time is it?" she heard her father mutter. Then she heard the faraway voice on the other end. She leaned against the kitchen counter with great relief. It was Griffin.

"Dad, I've got it. Sorry to wake you up."

"Huh?"

"Daddy, it's for me. Just hang up and go back to sleep." The phone clicked.

Phoebe clutched the receiver. "Griffin, I'm so glad to hear your voice. I was so worried. I thought you were going to call yesterday."

"Oh, yeah. I'm sorry," was all Griffin said. His voice was drained and flat. Phoebe had never heard him sound like that before.

"Griffin, is something wrong?"

"No," he said quickly. "Things are great. Really great." But his words were strained. There was an awkward pause.

"What happened with the show? Did you get it? Did you start rehearsals already?"

"Yeah."

Phoebe waited for Griffin to say more.

"Is it wonderful? Griffin, you sound kind of weird. What is it?"

"Oh, I'm just beat. You know, rehearsals and all. It's a lot."

"But it must be exciting. Isn't it?"

"It's great."

"Griffin, Sasha said I could say I was staying at her house tomorrow night. So that means I can go. We can be together. Griffin?" His silence was making her crazy.

"Uh, Phoebe, this is kind of strange I know, but. . . ."

"Yes?"

"I've been thinking about it and I'm not sure it's such a good idea for you to come and visit after all."

Phoebe caught her breath.

"Why not?"

Griffin exhaled loudly. "Well, to begin with, your folks don't know and everything . . ."

Phoebe couldn't believe it. Since when did Griffin concern himself with obeying parents? Never, since she had known him. He was the first one to fly off and follow his dream no matter what his own mother thought.

"They'll never know. Sasha and I planned the whole —"

"Phoebe, I don't want you to come."

"You —"

"Please try and understand." He spoke haltingly. "Things are changing so quickly for me and I think I have to break some ties with my old life. I have to give my new work all my attention."

"I won't distract you. Do you think I won't fit in with your New York friends? I don't. . . ."

"No, Phoebe that's not it. It's just —"

"What?"

"I love you. I'll always think about you. But we can't see each other anymore or talk or anything. I can't explain any more than that. I'm sorry."

Phoebe was no longer able to speak. The tears were washing down her face and her ribs were shaking with silent sobs. She was unable to form a single word.

"Phoebe. Phoebe, are you still there? Phoebe?"

Phoebe stared in front of her and slowly hung up the phone. She didn't understand. She never would. She loved Griffin more than she'd ever thought she could love anyone, and he had told her that it was over.

She wanted to talk to someone. She needed to talk to someone. It was too much to absorb all this by herself. But who could she call at this hour? Chris was probably still with Ted. Woody and Sasha would listen, but what would Phoebe say to them? That while they were out having a great time, she'd been crying until there wasn't a tear left in her? No, she couldn't spoil their homecoming that way. And there was probably nothing any of them could do for her right now anyway.

It was then that Phoebe realized whose comfort she really wanted — the one person who knew her so well, who had comforted her many times in the past.

"Brad," she whispered.

But even as Phoebe reached for the phone, she knew that she wouldn't do it. Calling Brad was out of the question. It wouldn't work. It wasn't fair. Brad had to find someone new.

Phoebe was alone.

There was someone else who had not attended the homecoming dance. She was also still awake on the clear fall night. Brenda Austin opened her second-story bedroom window and stared out at the stars. She heard a faint giggle and saw Ted's red MG in the shadow of a nearby porchlight. Ted and her stepsister were obviously still inside the car.

Brenda took a deep breath of cold air and wondered if she would ever get used to her new house, her new school, her new family. Sure, she had been in Rose Hill for more than a year, but she felt no more a part of it than she did in the days when she had first come.

A breeze lifted a tuft of Brenda's wavy dark hair and made her eyes water. She felt so alone. It was like most of the world was locked inside that red MG down there in the street, kept there for girls like Chris and safely guarded from girls like her.

Chris had no idea what really went on inside Brenda. If she did, she would never have suggested going to the dance with that guy Woody. How long must it have taken for Chris to have talked Woody into it? What a joke. Besides, Brenda didn't need some guy taking her to the dance as a favor to her stepsister. Even staying locked out of things forever would be better than that.

Brenda clenched her fist and leaned back against the wall next to her bed. What she really needed was someone who could understand, someone who knew what it was like to feel so angry and confused that running was the only solution. Was there anyone in Rose Hill who could understand her and what she had been through?

Leaning forward to peer out at the street again, Brenda took a deep, difficult breath. There had to be someone out there, she prayed to herself. There just had to be.

Coming soon...
Couples #3
Alone, Together

"Look," Brenda said finally, "I appreciate your concern and help, but why don't you go back to your friends? I'm sure that's what you've been wanting to do all along. I just want to be left alone."

Brad was not leaving. "Why don't we just go down the rest of this slope together? There's another steep section coming up."

"Go on! I don't need taking care of. I just want to be left alone. Go back to your friends!"

Suddenly Brad exploded. "What makes you think I want to go back to my friends?" he shouted. "Do you think you're the only person in the world who feels out of it?"

Brenda was stunned. His outburst shocked her out of her own humiliation. For a few moments it was very quiet.

Finally Brad pressed heel of his hand against

197

his forehead. "I'm sorry, I'm in a lousy mood. It has nothing to do with you."

Brenda stared at him. "I'm sorry."

"No, it was my fault. I should. . . ." Brad stopped in the middle of his sentence. "This is absurd," he said with a hint of a smile.

Brenda felt the sides of her mouth curl up. "I'm a pro at creating absurd situations."

Their eyes met and Brenda felt a little self-conscious. She started to shake the snow out of her hair. He watched her.

"Do you feel better? You're not dizzy or anything, are you?"

"No. I'm fine."

"You look okay. Actually you look better than okay." He now had a soft look in his eyes that sent a tingle all the way through her.

"Yeah, sure." Brenda laughed. She retied her bandana and emptied the caked snow that was wedged in the cuffs of her jeans.

"How about a ski lesson?" Brad suggested suddenly.

Brenda hesitated, "Well —"

"It can't be any worse than what just happened."

"I guess I could use a lesson."

"There's an intermediate slope on the other side. Do you want to try that?"

Brenda nodded.

"Go on ahead of me," Brad urged warmly. "I'll be right behind you if you fall."

Other books you will enjoy,
about real kids like you!

☐ MZ43124-2	**A Band of Angels** Julian F. Thompson	$2.95
☐ MZ40515-2	**City Light** Harry Mazer	$2.75
☐ MZ40943-3	**Fallen Angels** Walter Dean Myers	$3.50
☐ MZ40428-8	**I Never Asked You to Understand Me** Barthe DeClements	$2.75
☐ MZ43999-5	**Just a Romance** Ann M. Martin	$2.75
☐ MZ44629-0	**Last Dance** Caroline B. Cooney	$2.95
☐ MZ44628-2	**Life Without Friends** Ellen Emerson White	$2.95
☐ MZ43821-2	**A Royal Pain** Ellen Conford	$2.95
☐ MZ44626-6	**Saturday Night** Caroline B. Cooney	$2.95
☐ MZ44429-8	**A Semester in the Life of a Garbage Bag** Gordon Korman	$2.95
☐ MZ44770-X	**Seventeen and In-Between** Barthe DeClement	$2.75
☐ MZ41823-8	**Simon Pure** Julian F. Thompson	$2.75
☐ MZ41838-6	**Slam Book** Ann M. Martin	$2.75
☐ MZ43867-0	**Son of Interflux** Gordon Korman	$2.95
☐ MZ43817-4	**Three Sisters** Norma Fox Mazer	$2.95
☐ MZ41513-1	**The Tricksters** Margaret Mahy	$2.95
☐ MZ44773-3	**When the Phone Rang** Harry Mazer	$2.95

Available wherever you buy books, or use this order form.

Scholastic Inc., P.O. Box 7502, 2931 East McCarty Street, Jefferson City, MO 65102

Please send me the books I have checked above. I am enclosing $_____ (please add $2.00 to cover shipping and handling). Send check or money order — no cash or C.O.D.s please.

Name _____

Address _____

City _____ State/Zip _____

Please allow four to six weeks for delivery. Offer good in the U.S. only. Sorry, mail orders are not available to residents of Canada. Prices subject to change.   PNT1090

SUNFIRE®

**Read all about the fascinating young women who lived
and loved during America's most turbulent times!**

☐ MM32774-7	#1 **AMANDA**	Candice F. Ransom	**$2.95**
☐ MM33064-0	#2 **SUSANNAH**	Candice F. Ransom	**$2.95**
☐ MM33156-6	#4 **DANIELLE**	Vivian Schurfranz	**$2.95**
☐ MM33241-4	#5 **JOANNA**	Jane Claypool Miner	**$2.95**
☐ MM33242-2	#6 **JESSICA**	Mary Francis Shura	**$2.95**
☐ MM33239-3	#7 **CAROLINE**	Willo Davis Roberts	**$2.95**
☐ MM33433-6	#9 **MARILEE**	Mary Francis Shura	**$2.95**
☐ MM33381-X	#10 **LAURA**	Vivan Schurfranz	**$2.95**
☐ MM33410-7	#11 **EMILY**	Candice F. Ransom	**$2.95**
☐ MM33615-0	#13 **VICTORIA**	Willo Davis Roberts	**$2.95**
☐ MM33688-6	#14 **CASSIE**	Vivian Schurfranz	**$2.95**
☐ MM33686-X	#15 **ROXANNE**	Jane Claypool Miner	**$2.95**
☐ MM41468-2	#16 **MEGAN**	Vivian Schurfranz	**$2.75**
☐ MM41438-5	#17 **SABRINA**	Candice F. Ransom	**$2.75**
☐ MM42134-4	#18 **VERONICA**	Jane Claypool Miner	**$2.75**
☐ MM40049-5	#19 **NICOLE**	Candice F. Ransom	**$2.25**
☐ MM42021-6	#20 **JULIE**	Vivian Schurfranz	**$2.50**
☐ MM40394-X	#21 **RACHEL**	Vivian Schurfranz	**$2.50**
☐ MM43127-7	#22 **COREY**	Jane Claypool Miner	**$2.75**
☐ MM40717-1	#23 **HEATHER**	Vivian Schurfranz	**$2.50**
☐ MM43133-1	#24 **GABRIELLE**	Mary Francis Shura	**$2.75**
☐ MM41000-8	#25 **MERRIE**	Vivian Schurfranz	**$2.75**
☐ MM41012-1	#26 **NORA**	Jeffie Ross Gordon	**$2.75**
☐ MM41191-8	#27 **MARGARET**	Jane Claypool Miner	**$2.75**
☐ MM41207-8	#28 **JOSIE**	Vivian Schurfranz	**$2.75**
☐ MM41416-X	#29 **DIANA**	Mary Francis Shura	**$2.75**
☐ MM42043-7	#30 **RENEE**	Vivian Schurfranz	**$2.75**
☐ MM42015-1	#31 **JENNIE**	Jane Claypool Miner	**$2.75**

Available wherever you buy books, or use this order form.